The Werewolf of Fever Swamp

Just as I was about to pull open the crude wooden door, it swung out, nearly hitting us both. We leapt back as a man burst out from the dark doorway of the hut.

He glared at us with wild black eyes. He had long, grey-white hair, down past his shoulders, tied behind him in a loose ponytail.

His face was bright red, sunburned maybe. Or maybe red from anger. He stared at us with a menacing scowl, standing bent over, stooped from being inside the low hut . . .

As he glared at us with those amazing black eyes, his mouth opened, revealing rows of jagged yellow teeth.

Huddling close to my sister, I took a step back.

Goosebumps

The Werewolf of Fever Swamp

R.L. Stine

Hippo

Scholastic Children's Books,
Scholastic Publications Ltd,
7-9 Pratt Street, London NW1 0AE

Scholastic Inc.,
555 Broadway, New York, NY 10012-3999, USA

Scholastic Canada Ltd,
123 Newkirk Road, Richmond Hill,
Ontario, Canada L4C 3G5

Ashton Scholastic Pty Ltd,
P O Box 579, Gosford, New South Wales,
Australia

Ashton Scholastic Ltd,
Private Bag 92801, Penrose, Auckland,
New Zealand

First published in the US by Scholastic Inc., 1993
First published in the UK by Scholastic Publications Ltd, 1995

Text copyright © 1993 by Parachute Press

ISBN 0 590 55828 5

All rights reserved

Typeset by Contour Typesetters, Southall, London
Printed and bound in Great Britain by
Caledonian International Book Manufacturing Ltd, Glasgow
10 9 8 7 6

This book is sold subject to the condition that it shall not, by way of trade or
otherwise be lent, resold, hired out, or otherwise circulated without the
publisher's prior consent in any form of binding or cover other than that in
which it is published and without a similar condition, including this
condition, being imposed upon the subsequent purchaser.

We moved to Florida during the Christmas holidays. A week later, I heard the frightening howls in the swamp for the first time.

Night after night, the howls made me sit up in bed. I would hold my breath and wrap my arms around myself to keep from shivering.

I would stare out of my bedroom window at the chalk-coloured full moon. And I would listen.

What kind of creature makes such a cry? I would ask myself.

And how close is it? Why does it sound as if it's right outside my window?

The wails rose and fell like police car sirens. They weren't sad or mournful. They were menacing.

Angry.

They sounded to me like a warning. *Stay out of the swamp. You do not belong here.*

When my family first moved to Florida, to our new house at the edge of the swamp, I couldn't wait to explore. I stood in the back garden with the binoculars my dad had given me for my twelfth birthday and gazed towards the swamp.

Trees with slender, white trunks tilted over each other. Their flat, broad leaves appeared to form a roof, covering the swamp floor in blue shadow.

Behind me, the deer paced uneasily in their wire-mesh pen. I could hear them pawing the soft, sandy ground, rubbing their antlers against the walls of their pen.

Lowering my binoculars, I turned to look at them. The deer were the reason we had moved to Florida.

You see, my dad, Michael F. Tucker, is a scientist. He works for the University of Vermont in Burlington, which, believe me, is a *long* way from the Florida swamps!

Dad got six deer from some country in South America. They're called swamp deer. They're not like normal deer. I mean, they don't look like Bambi. For one thing, their fur is very red, not brown. And their hooves are really big and kind of webbed. For walking on wet, swampy ground, I suppose.

Dad wants to see if these South American swamp deer can survive in Florida. He plans to put little radio transmitters on them, and set them free in the swamp. Then he'll study how they get on.

When he told us back in Burlington that we were moving to Florida because of the deer, we all completely freaked out. We didn't want to move.

My sister, Emily, cried for days. She's sixteen, and she didn't want to miss her senior year in high school. I didn't want to leave my friends, either.

But Dad quickly got Mum on his side. Mum is a scientist, too. She and Dad work together on a lot of projects. So, of course, she agreed with him.

And the two of them tried to persuade Emily and me that this was the chance of a lifetime, that it was going to be really exciting. An adventure we'd never forget.

So here we were, living in a little white house in a neighbourhood of four or five other little white houses. We had six strange-looking red deer penned up behind the house. The hot Florida sun was beaming down. And an endless swamp stretched beyond our flat, grassy back garden.

I turned away from the deer and raised the binoculars to my face. "Oh," I cried out as two dark eyes seemed to be staring back at me.

I pulled the binoculars away and squinted towards the swamp. In the near distance I saw a large white bird on two long, spindly legs.

"It's a crane," Emily said. I hadn't realized

Emily had stepped up beside me. She was wearing a sleeveless white T-shirt and short red denim shorts. My sister is tall and thin and very blonde. She looks a lot like a crane.

The bird turned and began high-stepping towards the swamp.

"Let's follow it," I said.

Emily made her pouting face, an expression we'd all seen a lot of since moving down here. "No chance. It's too hot."

"Aw, come on." I tugged her skinny arm. "Let's do some exploring, look around the swamp."

She shook her head, her white-blonde ponytail swinging behind her. "I really don't want to, Grady." She adjusted her sunglasses on her nose. "I'm waiting for the post."

Since we're so far from the nearest post office, we only get post twice a week. Emily had been spending most of her time waiting for it.

"Waiting for a love letter from Martin?" I asked with a grin. She hated it when I teased her about Martin, her boyfriend back in Burlington. So I teased her as often as I could.

"Maybe," she said. She reached out with both hands and messed up my hair. She knows I hate to have my hair messed up.

"Please?" I pleaded. "Come on, Emily. Just a short walk. Very short."

"Emily, take a short walk with Grady," Dad's

4

voice broke in. We turned to see him inside the deer pen. He had a clipboard in one hand and was going from deer to deer, taking notes. "Go ahead," he urged my sister. "You're not doing anything else."

"But, Dad—" Emily could whine with the best of them when she wanted.

"Go ahead, Em," Dad insisted. "It will be interesting. More interesting than standing around in the heat arguing with him."

Emily pushed the sunglasses up again. They kept slipping down her nose. "Well . . ."

"Great!" I cried. I was really excited. I'd never been in a real swamp before. "Let's go!" I grabbed my sister's hand and pulled.

Emily reluctantly followed, a fretful expression on her face. "I have a bad feeling about this," she muttered.

My shadow slanting behind me, I hurried towards the low, tilting trees. "Emily, what could go wrong?" I asked.

It was hot and wet under the trees. The air felt sticky against my face. The broad palm leaves were so low, I could almost reach up and touch them. They nearly blocked out the sun, but shafts of yellow light broke through, beaming down on the swamp floor like spotlights.

Scratchy weeds and fern leaves brushed against my bare legs. I wished I'd worn jeans instead of shorts. I kept close to my sister as we made our way along a narrow, winding trail. The binoculars, strapped around my neck, began to feel heavy against my chest. I should've left them at home, I realized.

"It's so noisy here," Emily complained, stepping over a decaying log.

She was right. The most surprising thing about the swamp was all the sounds.

A bird trilled from somewhere above. Another bird replied with a shrill whistle. Insects chirruped loudly all around us. I heard a steady *tap-tap-tap*, like someone hammering on wood. A woodpecker? Palm leaves crackled as they swayed. Slender tree trunks creaked. My sandals made *thup thup* sounds, sinking into the marshy ground as I walked.

"Hey, look," Emily said, pointing. She pulled off her dark glasses to see better.

We had come to a small, oval-shaped pond. The water was dark green, half-hidden in shade. Floating on top were white water lilies, bending gracefully over flat, green lily pads.

"Pretty," Emily said, brushing an insect off her shoulder. "I'm going to come back here with my camera and take pictures of this pond. Look at the great light."

I followed her gaze. The near end of the pond was darkened by long shadows. But light slanted down through the trees at the other end, forming what looked like a bright curtain that spilled on to the still pond water.

"It is quite pretty," I admitted. I wasn't really into ponds. I was more interested in wildlife.

I let Emily admire the pond and the water lilies a little longer. Then I headed around the pond and deeper into the swamp.

My sandals slapped over the wet ground. Up ahead, a swarm of tiny gnats, thousands of them, danced silently in a shaft of sunlight.

"Yuck," Emily muttered. "I hate gnats. It

makes me itchy just to look at them." She scratched her arms.

We turned away—and both saw something scamper behind a fallen, moss-covered log.

"Hey—what was *that*?" Emily cried, grabbing my elbow.

"An alligator!" I shouted. "A hungry alligator!"

She uttered a short, frightened cry.

I laughed. "What's your problem, Em? It was just some kind of lizard."

She squeezed my arm hard, trying to make me flinch. "You're a creep, Grady," she muttered. She scratched her arms again. "It's far too itchy in this swamp," she complained. "Let's go back."

"Just a little bit further," I pleaded.

"No. Come on. I really want to get back." She tried to pull me, but I backed out of her grasp. "Grady—"

I turned and started walking away from her, deeper into the swamp. I heard the *tap-tap-tap* again, directly overhead. The low palm leaves scraped against each other, shifting in a soft, wet breeze. The shrill chirruping of the insects grew louder.

"I'm going home and leaving you here," Emily threatened.

I ignored her and kept walking. I knew she was bluffing.

8

My sandals crackled over dried, brown palm leaves. Without turning around, I could hear Emily a few steps behind me.

Another little lizard scampered across the path, just in front of my sandals. It looked like a dark arrow, shooting into the underbrush.

The ground suddenly sloped upwards. We found ourselves climbing a low hill into bright sunlight. A clearing of some sort.

Beads of sweat ran down my cheeks. The air was so wet, I felt as if I were swimming.

At the top of the hill, we stopped to look around. "Hey—another pond!" I cried, running over fat, yellow swamp grass, hurrying up to the water's edge.

But this pond looked different.

The dark green water wasn't flat and smooth. Leaning over it, I could see that it was murky and thick, like split-pea soup. It made disgusting gurgling and plopping sounds as it churned.

I leaned down closer to get a better look.

"It's quicksand!" I heard Emily cry in horror.

And then two hands shoved me hard from behind.

As I started to fall into the bubbling green stew, the same hands grabbed my waist and pulled me back.

Emily giggled. "Gotcha!" she cried, holding on to me, keeping me from turning around and thumping her.

"Hey—let go!" I cried angrily. "You almost pushed me into *quicksand*! That's not funny!"

She laughed even more, then let me go. "It isn't quicksand, dummy," she muttered. "It's a bog."

"Huh?" I turned to stare into the gloppy green water.

"It's a bog. A peat bog," she repeated impatiently. "Don't you know anything?"

"What's a peat bog?" I asked, ignoring her insults. Emily the Know-It-All. She's always bragging about how she knows everything and I'm a stupid idiot. But she gets Bs in school, and I get As. So who's the clever one?

10

"We learned about this last year when we studied the wetlands and rainforests," she replied smugly. "The pond is thick because it has peat moss growing in it. The moss grows and grows. It absorbs twenty-five times its own weight in water."

"It's foul-looking," I said.

"Why don't you drink some and see how it tastes," she urged.

She tried to push me again, but I ducked and skirted away. "I'm not thirsty," I muttered. I realize it wasn't too clever, but it was the best reply I could think of.

"Let's get going," she said, wiping sweat off her forehead with her hand. "I'm really hot."

"Yeah. Okay," I reluctantly agreed. "This was a fun walk."

We turned away from the peat bog and started back down the hill. "Hey, look!" I cried, pointing to two black shadows floating high above us under a white cloud.

"Falcons," Emily said, shielding her eyes with one hand as she gazed up. "I *think* they're falcons. It's hard to see. They really are big."

We watched them soar out of sight. Then we continued down the hill, making our way carefully on the damp, sandy ground.

At the bottom of the hill, back under the deep shade of the trees, we stopped to catch our breath.

I was really sweating now. The back of my neck felt hot and itchy. I rubbed it with one hand, but it didn't seem to help.

The breeze had stopped. The air felt heavy. Nothing moved.

Loud cawing sounds made me glance up. Two enormous blackbirds peered down at us from a low branch of a cypress tree. They cawed again, as if telling us to go away.

"This way," Emily said with a sigh.

I followed her, feeling prickly and itchy all over. "I wish we had a swimming pool at our new house," I said. "I'd jump right in with my clothes on!"

We walked for several minutes. The trees grew thicker. The light grew dimmer. The path ended. We had to push our way through tall, leafy ferns.

"I—I don't think we've been here before," I stammered. "I don't think this is the right way."

We stared at each other, watching each other's face fill with fright.

We both realized we were lost. Completely lost.

"I don't *believe* this!" Emily shrieked.

Her loud shout made the two blackbirds flutter off their tree limb. They soared away, cawing angrily.

"What am I *doing* here?" she cried. Emily is not good in emergencies. When she got a flat tyre during one of her first driving lessons back home in Burlington, she jumped out of the car and ran away!

So I didn't exactly expect her to be calm and cool now. Since we were completely lost in the middle of a dark, hot swamp, I expected her to panic. And she did.

I'm the calm one in the family. I take after Dad. Cool and scientific. "Let's just work out the direction of the sun," I said, ignoring the fluttering in my chest.

"What sun?" Emily cried, throwing her hands up in despair.

It was really dark. The palm trees with their

wide leaves formed a pretty solid roof above us.

"Well, we could check out some moss," I suggested. The fluttering in my chest was growing stronger. "Isn't moss supposed to grow on the north side of trees?"

"East side, I think," Emily muttered. "Or is it the west?"

"I'm pretty sure it's the north," I insisted, gazing around.

"Pretty sure? What good is pretty sure?" Emily cried shrilly.

"Forget the moss," I said, rolling my eyes. "I'm not even sure what moss looks like."

We stared at each other for a long time.

"Didn't you used to carry a compass with you wherever you went?" Emily asked, sounding a little shaky.

"Yeah. When I was four," I replied.

"I can't believe we were so stupid," Emily wailed. "We should have worn one of the radio transmitters. You know. For the deer. Then Dad could track us down."

"I should have worn jeans," I muttered, noticing some tiny red bumps along my calf. Poison ivy? Some kind of rash?

"What should we do?" Emily asked impatiently, wiping sweat off her forehead with her hand.

"Go back up the hill, I suppose," I told her.

"There were no trees there. It was sunny. Once we see where the sun is, we can work out the direction to get back."

"But which way is the hill?" Emily demanded.

I spun around. Was it behind us? To our right? A cold chill ran down my back as I realized I wasn't sure.

I shrugged. "We're really lost," I murmured with a sigh.

"Let's go this way," Emily said, starting to walk away. "I just have a feeling this is the way. If we come to that bog, we'll know we're going the right way."

"And if we don't?" I demanded.

"We'll come to something else, maybe," she replied.

Brilliant.

But I didn't see any good in arguing with her. So I followed.

We walked in silence, the shrill ringing of the insects on all sides, the calls of birds startling us from above. After a short while, we pushed our way through a clump of tall, stiff reeds.

"Have we been here before?" Emily asked.

I couldn't remember. I pushed a reed away to step through and realized it had left something sticky on my hand. "Yuck!"

"Hey, look!" Emily's excited cry made me glance up from the sticky green gunk that clung to my hand.

15

The bog! It was right in front of us. The same bog we had stopped at before.

"Yes!" Emily cried. "I *knew* I was right. I just had a feeling."

The sight of the gurgling green pond cheered us both up. Once past it, we began to run. We knew we were on the right path, nearly home.

"Brilliant!" I cried happily, running past my sister. "Brill!"

I was feeling really good again.

Then something reached up, grabbed my ankle, and pulled me down to the swampy ground.

I hit the ground hard, landing on my elbows and knees.

My heart leapt into my mouth.

I tasted blood.

"Get up! Get up!" Emily was screaming.

"It—it's *got* me!" I cried in a tight, trembling voice.

The fluttering in my chest had become a pounding. Again, I tasted blood.

I raised my eyes to see Emily laughing.

Laughing?

"It's just a tree root," she said, pointing.

I followed the direction of her finger—and instantly realized I hadn't been pulled down. I had tripped over one of the many upraised tree roots that arched over the ground.

I stared at the bonelike root. It was bent in the middle and looked like a skinny, white leg.

But what was the blood I tasted?

I felt my aching lip. I had bitten it when I fell.

With a loud groan, I pulled myself to my feet. My knees ached. My lip throbbed. Blood trickled down my chin.

"That was clumsy," Emily said softly. And then she added, "Are you okay?" She brushed some dried leaves off the back of my T-shirt.

"Yeah, I suppose so," I replied, still feeling a little shaky. "I really thought something had grabbed me." I forced a laugh.

She rested a hand on my shoulder, and we started walking again, slower than before, side by side.

Slender beams of light poked down through the thick tree leaves, dotting the ground in front of us. It all looked unreal, like something in a dream.

A creature scampered noisily behind the tangle of low shrubs to our right. Emily and I didn't even turn to try to see it. We just wanted to get home.

It didn't take us long to realize we were heading in the wrong direction.

We stopped at the edge of a small, round clearing. Birds chattered noisily above us. A light breeze made the palm leaves scrape and creak.

"What are those huge grey things?" I asked, lingering behind my sister.

"Mushrooms, I think," she replied quietly.

"Mushrooms as big as footballs," I murmured.

We both saw the small shack at the same time.

It was hidden in the shadow of two low cypress trees beyond the field of giant mushrooms at the other side of the clearing.

We both gaped at it in surprise, studying it in shocked silence. We took a few steps towards it. Then a few more.

The shack was tiny, built low to the ground, not much taller than me. It had some kind of thatched roof, made of long reeds or dried grass. The walls were made of layers of dried palm leaves.

The door, built of slender tree limbs bound together, was shut tight. There were no windows.

A pile of grey ashes formed a circle a few metres from the door. Signs of a campfire.

I saw a pair of battered old workboots lying at the side of the shack. Beside them were several empty tin cans on their sides and a plastic water bottle, also empty, partly crumpled.

I turned to Emily and whispered, "Do you think someone lives here? In the middle of the swamp?"

She shrugged, her features tight with fear.

"If someone lives here, maybe he can tell us which way to go to get home," I suggested.

"Maybe," Emily murmured. Her eyes were staring straight ahead at the tiny shack covered in blue shadow.

We took another couple of steps closer.

Why would someone want to live in a tiny shack like this in the middle of a swamp? I wondered.

An answer flashed into my mind: Because whoever it is wants to hide from the world.

"It's a hideout," I muttered, not realizing I was speaking out loud. "A criminal. A bank robber. Or a *killer*. He's hiding here."

"*Sshhh.*" Emily put a finger on my mouth to silence me, hitting the cut on my lip. I pulled away.

"Anyone home?" she called. Her voice came out low and shaky, so low I could barely hear her. "Anyone home?" she repeated, a little more forcefully.

I decided to join in. We shouted together: "Anyone home? Anyone in there?"

We listened.

No reply.

We stepped up to the low door.

"Anyone in there?" I called one more time.

Then I reached for the doorknob.

Just as I was about to pull open the crude wooden door, it swung out, nearly hitting us both. We leapt back as a man burst out from the dark doorway of the hut.

He glared at us with wild black eyes. He had long, grey-white hair, down past his shoulders, tied behind him in a loose ponytail.

His face was bright red, sunburned maybe. Or maybe red from anger. He stared at us with a menacing scowl, standing bent over, stooped from being inside the low hut.

He wore a loose-fitting white T-shirt, dirt-stained and wrinkled, over heavy black trousers that bagged over his sandals.

As he glared at us with those amazing black eyes, his mouth opened, revealing rows of jagged yellow teeth.

Huddling close to my sister, I took a step back.

I wanted to ask him who he was, why he lived

in the swamp. I wanted to ask if he could help us find our way back home.

A dozen questions flashed through my mind. But all I could utter was, "Uh . . . sorry."

Then I realized that Emily was already running away. Her ponytail flew behind her as she dived through the tall weeds.

And a second later, I was running after her. My heart pounded. My sandals squashed over the soft ground.

"Hey, Emily—wait for me! Wait for me!"

I ran over the rough carpet of dead leaves and twigs.

As I struggled to catch up with her, I glanced behind me—and cried out in terror. "Emily—he's *chasing* us!"

Bent low to the ground, the man from the hut
moved steadily after us, taking long strides. His
hands bobbed at his sides. He was breathing
hard, and his mouth was open, revealing jagged
teeth.

"Run!" Emily cried. "Run, Grady!"

We were following a narrow path between tall
weeds. The trees thinned out. We ran through
shadow and sunlight and back into shadow.

"Emily—wait for me!" I called breathlessly.
But she didn't slow down.

A long, narrow pond appeared to our left.
Strange trees lifted up from the middle of the
water. The slender trunks were surrounded by a
thicket of dark roots. Mangrove trees.

I wanted to stop and look at the eerie-looking
trees. But this wasn't the time for sightseeing.

We ran along the edge of the pond, our sandals
sinking into the marshy ground. Then, my
chest heaving, my throat choked and dry,

I followed Emily as the path curved into the trees.

A sharp pain in my side made me cry out. I stopped running. I gasped for breath.

"Hey—he's gone," Emily said, swallowing hard. She stopped a few metres in front of me and leaned against a tree trunk. "We lost him."

I bent over, trying to force away the pain in my side. After a short while, my breathing slowed to normal. "Weird," I said. I couldn't think of anything else.

"Yeah. Weird," Emily agreed. She walked back to me and pulled me up straight. "You okay?"

"I think so." At least the pain had faded away. I always get a pain in my right side when I run for a long time. This one was worse than usual. I usually don't have to run for my life!

"Come on," Emily said. She let go of me and started walking quickly, following the path.

"Hey, this looks familiar," I said. I began to feel a little better. I started to jog. We passed clusters of trees and ferns that looked familiar. I could see our footprints in the sandy ground, going the other way.

A short while later, our back garden came into view. "Home sweet home!" I cried.

Emily and I stepped out from the low trees and began running across the grass towards the back of the house.

Mum and Dad were in the back garden setting up outdoor furniture. Dad was lowering an umbrella into the white umbrella table. Mum was washing off the white lawn chairs with the garden hose.

"Hey—welcome back," Dad said, smiling.

"We thought you'd got lost," Mum said.

"We did!" I cried breathlessly.

Mum turned off the nozzle, stopping the spray of water. "You *what*?"

"A man chased us!" Emily exclaimed. "A strange man with long white hair."

"He lives in a hut. In the middle of the swamp," I added, dropping down into one of the lawn chairs. It was wet, but I didn't care.

"Huh? He chased you?" Dad's eyes narrowed in alarm. Then he said, "I heard in town there's a swamp hermit out there."

"Yes, he chased us!" Emily repeated. Her normally pale face was bright red. Her hair had come loose and fell wildly around her face. "It—it was scary."

"A man in the hardware shop told me about him," Dad said. "Said he was strange, but perfectly harmless. No one knows his name."

"Harmless?" Emily cried. "Then why did he chase us?"

Dad shrugged. "I'm only repeating what I heard. Evidently he's lived in the swamp most of his life. By himself. He never comes into town."

Mum dropped the hose and walked over to Emily. She placed a hand on Emily's shoulder. In the bright sunlight, they looked like sisters. They're both tall and thin, with long, straight blonde hair. I look more like my dad. Wavy brown hair. Dark eyes. A little chunky.

"Maybe they shouldn't go back in the swamp by themselves," Mum said, biting her lower lip fretfully. She started to gather Emily's hair back up into a ponytail.

"The hermit is supposed to be completely harmless," Dad repeated. He was still struggling to lower the umbrella into the concrete base. Every time he lowered it, he missed the opening.

"Here, Dad. I'll help you." I scooted under the table and guided the umbrella stem into the base.

"Don't worry," Emily said. "You won't catch *me* back in that swamp." She scratched both shoulders. "I'm going to be itchy for the rest of my life!" she groaned.

"We saw a lot of cool things," I said, starting to feel normal again. "A peat bog and mangrove trees . . ."

"I told you this was going to be an experience," Dad said, arranging the white chairs around the table.

"Some experience," Emily grumbled, rolling her eyes. "I'm going in to have a shower. Maybe if I stay in it for an hour or so, I'll stop itching."

Mum shook her head, watching Emily march towards the back door. "This is going to be a hard year for Em," she muttered.

Dad wiped his dirty hands on the sides of his jeans. "Come with me, Grady," he said, motioning for me to follow him. "Time to feed the deer."

We talked more about the swamp at dinner. Dad told us stories about how they hunted and trapped the swamp deer that he was using for his experiment.

Dad and his helpers searched the South American jungles for weeks. They used tranquillizer guns to capture the deer. Then they had to bring in helicopters to pull the deer out, and the deer were not too happy about flying.

"The swamp you two were exploring this afternoon," he said, twirling his spaghetti. "Know what it's called? Fever Swamp. That's what the local people call it, anyway."

"Why?" Emily asked. "Because it's so hot in there?"

Dad chewed and swallowed a mouthful of spaghetti. He had orange splodges of tomato sauce on both sides of his mouth. "I don't know why it's called Fever Swamp. But I'm sure we'll find out eventually."

"It was probably discovered by a man named

Mr Fever," Mum joked.

"I want to go home to Vermont!" Emily wailed.

After dinner, I found myself feeling a little homesick, too. I took a tennis ball out to the back of the house. I thought maybe I could bounce it off the wall and catch it the way I had done back home.

But the deer pen was in the way.

I thought about my two best friends back in Burlington, Ben and Adam. We had lived on the same street and used to go out together after dinner. We'd throw a ball around or walk down to the playground and just mess around.

Staring at the deer, who milled silently at one end of the pen, I realized I really missed my friends. I wondered what they were doing right now. Probably hanging around in Ben's back garden.

Feeling glum, I was about to go back inside and see what was on TV—when a hand grabbed me from behind.

The swamp hermit!

He's found me!

The swamp hermit has found me! And now he's got me!

Those are the thoughts that burst into my mind.

I spun around—and uttered a startled cry when I saw that it wasn't the swamp hermit. It was a boy.

"Hi," he said. "I thought you saw me. I didn't mean to scare you." He had a funny voice, gravelly and hoarse.

"Oh. Uh . . . that's okay," I stammered.

"I saw you in your garden," he said. "I live over there." He pointed to the house two doors down. "You just moved in?"

I nodded. "Yeah. I'm Grady Tucker." I slapped the tennis ball into my hand. "What's your name?"

"Will. Will Blake," he said in his hoarse voice. He was about my height, but he was heavier, bigger somehow. His shoulders were broader. His neck was thicker. He reminded me of a wrestler.

He had dark brown hair, cut very short. It stood straight up on top, like a flat-top, and was swept back on the sides. He wore a blue-and-white-striped T-shirt and denim cut-offs.

"How old are you?" he asked.

"Twelve," I answered.

"Me, too," he told me, glancing over my shoulder at the deer. "I thought maybe you were eleven. I mean, you look quite young."

I was insulted by that remark, but I decided to ignore it. "How long have you lived here?" I asked, tossing the tennis ball from hand to hand.

"A few months," Will said.

"Are there any other kids our age?" I asked, glancing down the row of six houses.

"Yeah. One," Will replied. "But she's a girl. And she's weird."

In the distance, the sun was lowering itself behind the swamp trees. The sky was a dark scarlet. The air suddenly became cooler. Gazing high in the sky, I could see a pale moon, nearly full.

Will headed over to the deer pen, and I followed him. He walked heavily, his big shoulders bobbing with each step. He poked his hand through the wire mesh and let a deer lick his palm.

"Your father works for the Forest Service, too?" he asked, his eyes studying the deer.

"No," I told him. "My mum and dad are both scientists. They're doing studies with these deer."

"Weird-looking deer," Will said. He pulled his wet hand from the pen and held it up. "Yuck. Deer slime."

I laughed. "They're called swamp deer," I told him. I tossed him the tennis ball. We backed away from the deer pen and started to throw the ball back and forth.

"Have you been in the swamp?" he asked.

I missed the ball and had to chase it across the grass. "Yeah. This afternoon," I told him. "My sister and I, we got lost."

He sniggered.

"Do you know why it's called Fever Swamp?" I asked, tossing him a high one.

It was getting quite dark, harder to see. But he caught the ball one-handed. "Yeah. My dad told me the story," Will said. "I think it was a hundred years ago. Maybe longer. Everyone in town came down with a strange fever."

"Everyone?" I asked.

He nodded. "Everyone who had been in the swamp." He held on to the ball and moved closer. "My dad said the fever lasted for weeks, sometimes even months. And lots of people died from it."

"That's horrible," I murmured, glancing across the back garden to the darkening trees at the swamp edge.

"And those who didn't die from the fever began acting very strange," Will continued. He had small, round eyes. And as he told his story, his eyes gleamed. "They started talking nonsense, not making any sense, just saying silly words. And they couldn't walk very well. They'd fall down a lot or walk around in circles."

"Weird," I said, my eyes still trained on the swamp. The sky darkened from scarlet to a deep purple. The nearly full moon seemed to glow brighter.

"Ever since that time, they've called it Fever Swamp," Will said, finishing his story. He flipped the tennis ball to me. "I'd better get home."

"Did you ever see the swamp hermit?" I asked.

He shook his head. "No. I've heard about him, but I've never seen him."

"I have," I told him. "My sister and I saw him this afternoon. We found his hut."

"That's cool!" Will exclaimed. "Did you talk to him or anything?"

"No way," I replied. "He chased us."

"He did?" Will's expression turned thoughtful. "Why?"

"I don't know. We were pretty scared," I admitted.

"I've got to go," Will said. He started jogging towards his house. "Hey, maybe you and I can go exploring in the swamp together," he called back.

"Yeah. Great!" I replied.

I felt a little cheered up. I'd made a new friend. Maybe it won't be so bad living here, I thought.

I watched Will head around the side of his house two doors down. His house looked almost identical to ours, except there was no deer pen in the back, of course.

I saw a set of swings with a small slide and seesaw in his back garden. I wondered if he had a little brother or sister.

I thought about Emily as I headed for the house. I knew she'd be jealous that I'd made a friend. Poor Emily was really sad without that idiot Martin hanging around her.

I never liked Martin. He always called me "Kiddo".

I watched one of the deer lower itself to the ground, folding its legs gracefully. Another deer did the same. They were settling down for the night.

I made my way inside and joined my family in the living room. They were watching a programme about sharks on the Discovery Channel.

My parents *love* the Discovery Channel. Big surprise, huh?

I watched for a short while. Then I began to realize I wasn't feeling very well. I had a headache, a sharp throbbing at my temples. And I felt chilly.

I told Mum. She got up and walked over to my chair. "You look a little flushed," she said, studying me with concern. She placed a cool hand on my forehead and left it there for a few seconds.

"Grady, I think you have a slight temperature," she said.

A few nights later, I heard the strange, frightening howls for the first time.

My temperature had gone up to 101 degrees and stayed there for a day. Then it went away. Then it came back.

"It's the swamp fever!" I told my parents earlier that night. "Pretty soon I'm going to start going crazy."

"You're already going crazy," Mum teased. She handed me a glass of orange juice. "Drink. Keep drinking."

"Drinking won't help swamp fever," I insisted glumly, taking the glass anyway. "There's no cure for it."

Mum tsk-tsked. Dad continued to read his science magazine.

I had strange dreams that night, disturbing dreams. I was back in Vermont, running through the snow. Something was chasing me. I thought maybe it was the swamp hermit. I kept running and running. I was very cold. I was shivering in the dream.

I turned back to see who was chasing me. There wasn't anyone there. And suddenly, I was in the swamp. I was sinking in a peat bog. It gurgled all around me, green and thick, making sick sucking sounds.

It was sucking me down. Down . . .

The howls woke me up.

I sat straight up in my bed and stared out of the window at the nearly full moon. It floated right beyond the window, silvery and bright against the blue-black sky.

Another long howl rose on the night air.

I realized I was shaking all over. I was sweating. My pyjama top was stuck to my back.

Gripping the covers with both hands, I listened hard.

Another howl. The cry of an animal.

From the swamp?

The cries sounded so close. Right outside the window. Long, angry howls.

I shoved down the covers and lowered my feet to the floor. I was still trembling and my head throbbed as I stood up. I reckoned I still had a temperature.

Another long howl.

I made my way to the hall on shaky legs. I had to find out if my parents had heard the howls, too.

Walking through the darkness, I bumped into a low table in the corridor. I still wasn't used to this new house.

My feet were cold as ice, but my head felt burning hot, as if it were on fire. Rubbing the knee I had banged, I waited for my eyes to adjust to the darkness. Then I continued down the corridor.

My parents' room was just past the kitchen at the back of the house. I was halfway across the kitchen when I stopped short.

What was that sound?

A scratching sound.

My breath caught in my throat. I froze, my arms stiff at my sides.

I listened.

There it was again.

Over the pounding of my heart, I heard it.

Scratch scratch scratch.

Someone—or some*thing*—scratching at the kitchen door.

Then—another howl. So close. So terrifyingly close.

Scratch scratch scratch.

What could it be? Some kind of animal? Just outside the house?

Some kind of swamp animal howling and scratching at the door?

I realized I'd been holding my breath a long while. I let it out in a *whoosh*, then sucked in another breath.

I listened hard, straining to hear over the pounding of my heart.

The fridge clicked on. The loud click nearly made me jump out of my skin. I grabbed the table. My hands were as cold as my feet, cold and clammy.

I listened.

Scratch scratch scratch.

I took a step towards the kitchen door.

One step, then I stopped.

A shudder of fear ran down my back.

I realized I wasn't alone.

Someone was there, breathing beside me in the dark kitchen.

I gasped. I was gripping the table so hard, my hand ached.

"Wh-who's there?" I whispered.

The kitchen light flashed on.

"Emily!" I practically shouted her name, in surprise and relief. "Emily—"

"Did you hear the howls?" she asked, speaking just above a whisper. Her blue eyes burned into mine.

"Yes. They woke me up," I said. "They sound so angry."

"Like a cry of attack," Emily whispered. "Why do you look so weird, Grady?"

"Huh?" Her question caught me off guard.

"Your face is all red," she said. "And look at you—you're all shaky."

"I think my temperature's back," I told her.

"Swamp fever," she murmured, examining me with her eyes. "Maybe it's the swamp fever you were telling me about."

I turned to the kitchen door. "Did you hear the scratching sounds?" I asked. "Something was scratching at the back door."

"Yes," she whispered. She stared at the door.

We both listened.

Silence.

"Do you think one of the deer escaped?" she asked, taking a few steps towards the door, her arms crossed in front of her pink-and-white robe.

"Do you think a deer would scratch at the door?" I asked.

It was such a silly question, we both burst out laughing.

"Maybe it wanted a glass of water!" Emily exclaimed, and we both laughed again. Giddy laughter. Nervous laughter.

We both cut our laughter short at the same time, and listened.

Another howl rose up outside like a police siren.

I saw Emily's eyes narrow in fear. "It's a wolf!" she cried in a hushed whisper. She raised a hand to her mouth. "Only a wolf makes a sound like that, Grady."

"Emily, come on—" I started to protest.

"No. I'm right," she insisted. "It's a wolf howl."

"Em, stop," I said, sinking on to a kitchen stool. "There are no wolves in the Florida swamps. You can look in the guidebooks. Or

40

better yet, ask Mum and Dad. Wolves don't live in swamps."

She started to argue, but a scratching at the door made her stop.

Scratch scratch scratch.

We both heard it. We both reacted with sharp gasps.

"What *is* that?" I whispered. And then, reading her expression, I quickly added, "Don't say it's a wolf."

"I—I don't know," she replied, both hands raised to her face. I recognized her look of panic. "Let's get Mum and Dad."

I grabbed the doorknob. "Let's just take a look," I said.

I don't know where my sudden courage came from. Maybe it was the fever. But, suddenly, I just wanted to solve the mystery.

Who or what was scratching at the door?

There was one good way to find out—open the door and look outside.

"No, Grady—wait!" Emily pleaded.

But I waved away her protests.

Then I turned the doorknob and pulled open the kitchen door.

A gust of hot, wet air rushed in through the open door. The chirp of cicadas greeted my ears.

Holding on to the door, I peered into the darkness of the back garden.

Nothing.

The nearly full moon, yellow as a lemon, floated high in the sky. Thin wisps of black clouds drifted over it.

The cicadas stopped suddenly, and all was quiet.

Too quiet.

I squinted into the distance, towards the blackness of the swamp.

Nothing moved. Nothing made a sound.

I waited for my eyes to adjust to the darkness. The moonlight sent a pale glow over the grass. In the far distance, I could see the black outline of slanting trees where the swamp began.

Who or what had scratched at the door? Were they hiding in the darkness now?

Watching me?

Waiting for me to close the door so they could begin their frightening howls again?

"Grady—close the door."

I could hear my sister's voice behind me. She sounded so frightened.

"Grady—can you see something? Can you?"

"No," I told her. "Just the moon."

I ventured out on to the back step. The air was hot and steamy, like the air in the bathroom after you've taken a hot shower.

"Grady—come back. Close the door." Emily's voice was shrill and trembly.

I gazed towards the deer pen. I could see their shadowy forms, still and silent. The hot wind rustled the grass. The cicadas began chirping again.

"Is anybody out there?" I called. I immediately felt foolish.

There was no one out there.

"Grady—shut the door. Now."

I felt Emily's hand on my pyjama sleeve. She tugged me back into the kitchen. I closed the door and locked it.

My face felt wet from the damp night air. I felt shivery. My knees were shaking.

"You look sick," Emily said. She glanced over my shoulder to the door. "Did you see anything?"

"No," I told her. "Nothing. It's so dark out there, even with a full moon."

"What's going on in here?" A stern voice interrupted us. Dad lumbered into the kitchen, adjusting the collar of the long nightshirt he always wore. "It's past midnight." He glanced from Emily to me, then back to Emily, looking for a clue.

"We heard noises," Emily said. "Howls outside."

"And then something was scratching at the door," I added, trying to keep my knees from shaking.

"Fever dreams," Dad said to me. "Look at you. You're as red as a tomato. And you're shaking. Let's take your temperature. You must be burning up." He started towards the bathroom to get the thermometer.

"It wasn't a dream," Emily called after him. "I heard the noises, too."

Dad stopped in the doorway. "Did you check the deer?"

"Yeah. They're okay," I said.

"Then maybe it was just the wind. Or some creatures in the swamp. It's hard to sleep in a new house. The sounds are all so new, so unfamiliar. But you'll both get used to them after a while."

I'll *never* get used to those horrible howls, I thought stubbornly. But I headed back to my room.

Dad took my temperature. It was just slightly

44

above normal. "You should be fine by to-morrow," he said, smoothing my blanket over me. "No more wandering around tonight, okay?"

I murmured a reply and almost instantly drifted into a restless sleep.

Again I had strange, troubling dreams. I dreamed I was walking in the swamp. I heard the howls. I could see the full moon between the slender tree trunks of the swamp.

I started to run. And then suddenly I was up to my waist in a thick, green bog. And the howls continued, one after the other, echoing through the trees as I sank into the murky bog.

When I awoke the next morning, the dream lingered in my mind. I wondered if the howls were real, or just part of the dream.

Climbing out of bed, I realized I felt fine. Yellow morning sunlight poured in through the window. I could see a clear blue sky. The beautiful morning made me forget my night-mares.

I wondered if Will was around this morning. Maybe he and I could go exploring in the swamp.

I got dressed quickly, pulling on pale blue jeans and a black-and-silver Raiders T-shirt. (I'm not a Raiders fan. I just like their colours.)

I gulped down a bowl of Frosties, allowed my

mum to feel my head to make sure my temperature had gone, and hurried to the back door.

"Whoa. Hold on," Mum called, putting down her coffee cup. "Where are you going so early?"

"I want to see if Will is at home," I said. "Maybe we'll go somewhere together or something."

"Okay. Just don't overdo it," she warned. "Promise?"

"Yeah. Promise," I replied.

I pulled open the kitchen door, stepped out into blinding sunlight—and screamed as an enormous, dark monster leapt on to my chest and heaved me to the ground.

"It—it's *got* me!" I screamed as it pushed me to the ground and jumped on my chest.

"Help! It—it's *licking my face!*"

I was so startled, it took me a long time to realize my attacker was a dog.

By the time Mum and Dad came to my rescue and started to pull the big creature off my chest, I was laughing. "Hey—that tickles! Stop!"

I wiped the dog spit off my face with my hands and scrambled to my feet.

"Where'd *you* come from?" Mum asked the dog. She and Dad were holding on to the enormous beast.

They both let go, and it stood wagging its tail excitedly, panting, its big red tongue hanging down practically to the ground.

"He's enormous!" Dad exclaimed. "He must be part German shepherd."

I was still wiping the sticky saliva off my

cheeks. "He scared me to death," I confessed. "Didn't you, fella?" I reached down and stroked the dark grey fur on the top of his head. His long tail started wagging faster.

"He likes you," Mum said.

"He practically *killed* me!" I exclaimed. "Look at him. He must weigh more than fifty kilos!"

"Were *you* the one scratching at our door last night?" Emily appeared in the doorway, still in the long T-shirt she used as a nightshirt. "I think this clears up the mystery," she said to me, yawning sleepily and pulling her blonde hair behind her shoulders with both hands.

"I suppose so," I muttered. I got down on my knees beside the big dog and stroked his back. He turned his head and licked my cheek again. "Yuck! Stop that!" I told him.

"I wonder who he belongs to?" Mum said, staring at the dog thoughtfully. "Grady, check his collar. There's probably an ID tag."

I reached up to the dog's broad neck and felt around in his fur for a collar. "Nothing there," I reported.

"Maybe he's a stray," Emily said from inside the kitchen. "Maybe that's why he was scratching the door last night."

"Yeah," I said quickly. "He needs a place to live."

"Whoa," Mum said, shaking her head. "I don't

think we need a dog right now, Grady. We've only just moved in, and—"

"But I *need* a pet!" I insisted. "It's so lonely here. A dog would be great, Mum. He could keep me company."

"You have the deer for pets," Dad said, frowning. He turned to the deer pen. The six deer were all standing alertly at attention, staring warily at the dog.

"You can't walk a deer!" I protested. "Besides, you're going to set the deer free, aren't you?"

"The dog probably belongs to someone," Mum said. "You can't just claim any dog that wanders past. Besides, he's so big, Grady. He's too big to—"

"Oh, let him keep it," Emily called from the house.

I stared at her in shock. I couldn't remember the last time Emily and I had been on the same side in a family argument.

The discussion continued for several minutes more. Everyone agreed that he seemed like a sweet-tempered, gentle dog despite his huge size. And he certainly was affectionate. I couldn't make him stop licking me.

Glancing up, I saw Will come out of his house and head across the back lawn towards us. He was wearing a sleeveless blue T-shirt and blue Lycra cycling shorts. "Hi! Look what we found!" I called.

I introduced Will to my mum and dad. Emily had disappeared back up to her room again to get dressed.

"Have you seen this dog before?" Dad asked Will. "Does he belong to someone in the area?"

Will shook his head. "Nope. Never seen him." He cautiously petted the dog's head.

"Where'd you come from, fella?" I asked, staring into the creature's eyes. They were blue. Sky-blue.

"He looks more like a wolf than a dog," Will said.

"Yeah. He really does," I agreed. "Was that you howling like a wolf all night?" I asked the dog. He tried to lick my nose, but I pulled my face back in time.

I glanced up at Will. "Did you hear those howls last night? They were really weird."

"No. I didn't hear anything," Will replied. "I'm a very sound sleeper. My dad comes into my room and shouts through a megaphone to wake me up in the morning. Really!"

We all laughed.

"He really *does* look like a wolf," Mum commented, staring at the dog's blue eyes.

"Wolves are skinnier," Dad remarked. "Their snouts are narrower. He could be *part* wolf, I suppose. But it's not very likely in this geographical area."

"Let's call him Wolf," I suggested enthusiastically. "It's the perfect name for him." I climbed to my feet. "Hi, Wolf," I called to the dog. "Wolf! Hi, Wolf!"

His ears perked straight up.

"See? He likes the name!" I exclaimed. "Wolf! Wolf!"

He barked at me, a single yip.

"Can I keep him?" I asked.

Mum and Dad exchanged long glances. "We'll see," Mum said.

That afternoon, Will and I headed off to the swamp to do some exploring. My nightmares about the swamp lingered in my mind. But I did my best to force them away.

It was a blazing hot day. The sun burned down in a clear, cloudless sky. As we crossed my back garden, I hoped it would be cooler in the leafy shade of the swamp.

I glanced back at Wolf. He was napping on his side in the hot sunlight, his four legs stretched straight out in front of him.

We had fed him before lunch, some leftover roast beef scraps from our dinner the night before. He gobbled it up hungrily. Then, after slurping up an entire bowl of water, he dropped down in the grass in front of the back door to take his nap.

Will and I followed the dirt path into the slanting trees. Black-and-orange monarch

51

butterflies, four or five of them, fluttered over a bank of tall wildflowers.

"Hey!" I cried out as my foot sank into a marshy spot in the dirt. When I pulled my trainer out, it was covered with wet sand.

"Have you seen the bog?" Will asked. "It's really cool."

"Yeah. Let's go there," I said enthusiastically. "We can throw sticks in and stuff, and watch them sink."

"Do you think any people ever got stuck in the bog?" Will asked thoughtfully. He brushed a mosquito off his broad forehead, then scratched his short, dark brown hair.

"Maybe," I replied, following him as he turned off the path and headed through a wide patch of tall reeds. "Do you think it would really suck you down into it, like quicksand?"

"My dad says there's no such thing as quicksand," Will said.

"I bet there is," I told him. "I bet people have fallen into the bog accidentally and were sucked down. If we brought a fishing rod, we could cast a line in and pull up their bones."

"Disgusting," he said.

We were walking over a carpet of dead brown leaves. Our trainers crunched noisily as we made our way under tangled palm trees towards the bog.

Suddenly, Will stopped. "*Ssshhh.*" He raised a finger to his lips.

I heard it, too.

Crunching behind us.

Footsteps.

We both froze in place, listening hard. The footsteps grew closer.

Will's dark eyes narrowed in fear. "Someone's following us," he murmured. "It's the swamp hermit!"

"Quick—hide!" I cried.

Will dived behind a thick clump of tall weeds. I tried to follow him, but there wasn't room for both of us.

Crawling on my hands and knees, I searched frantically for something to hide behind.

The crackling of dead leaves became louder. The footsteps hurried closer.

I scrambled towards a nest of brambles. No. They wouldn't hide me.

A clump of ferns opposite me was too low.

The footsteps crackled closer.

Closer.

"Hide! Hide!" Will urged.

But I was trapped out in the open. Caught.

I struggled to my feet just as our pursuer came into view.

"Wolf!" I cried.

The big dog's tail began wagging furiously as

soon as he saw me. He uttered a joyful bark—
and jumped.

"No!" I managed to cry.

His front paws landed hard on my chest. I
stumbled backwards into the tall weeds and fell
on to Will.

"Hey!" He cried out and scrambled to his
feet.

Wolf barked happily and practically
smothered me, trying to lick my face.

"Wolf—down! Down!" I shouted. I stood up
and started brushing dead leaves off my T-shirt.
"Wolf, you've got to stop doing that, boy," I told
him. "You're not a little puppy, you know."

"How did he find us?" Will asked, pulling a
burr off the seat of his blue Lycra shorts.

"Good nose, I suppose," I replied, staring
down at the happily panting dog. "Maybe he's
part hunting dog or something."

"Let's get to the bog," Will said impatiently.
He began leading the way, but Wolf pushed past
him, nearly bumping him over, and continued
trotting towards the bog, his powerful legs
taking long, steady strides.

"Wolf acts as if he knows where we're going," I
said, a little surprised.

"Maybe he's been here before," Will replied.
"Maybe he's a swamp dog."

"Maybe," I replied thoughtfully, staring down
at Wolf. Where *do* you come from, dog? I

wondered. He certainly did seem at home in the swamp.

In a short while, we came to the edge of the peat bog. I wiped the sweat off my forehead with the back of my hand and stared across the oval-shaped pond.

Shafts of sunlight made the green surface sparkle. Thousands of tiny white insects fluttered just above it, catching the light, glistening like little diamonds.

Will picked up a small tree branch. He cracked it in half between his hands. Then he heaved one of the halves high into the air.

It hit the surface of the bog with more of a *thunk* than a *splash*. And then it just lay there. It didn't sink.

"Weird," I said. "Let's try something heavier."

I started to search for something, but a low growl caught my attention. I turned towards the sound. To my surprise, it was coming from Wolf.

The dog had lowered its big head. Its entire body stood tensed, as if in attack position. Its dark lips were pulled back, revealing two sharp rows of teeth. It uttered a low growl, then another.

"I think he senses danger," Will said softly.

14

Wolf uttered another menacing growl, baring his jagged teeth. The fur on his back stood up stiffly. His legs tensed as if preparing to attack.

The sound of crackling twigs made me raise my eyes. I saw a grey figure darting behind tall weeds on the other side of the bog.

"Who—who's that?" Will whispered.

I stared straight ahead, unable to speak.

"Is that—" Will started.

"Yes," I managed to choke out. "It's him. The swamp hermit." I dropped quickly to my knees, hoping to keep out of view.

But had he already seen us?

Had he been there at the other side of the bog all along?

Will must have been sharing my thoughts. "Has that weirdo been *spying* on us?" he demanded, huddling beside me.

Wolf uttered a quiet growl, still frozen in place, ready to attack.

Keeping low, I scooted closer to the dog. For protection, I suppose.

I watched the strange man as he made his way through the weeds. His long grey-white hair was wild, standing straight out around his face. He kept glancing behind him as he walked, as if making sure he wasn't being followed.

He carried a brown sack over one shoulder.

He turned his gaze in our direction. I dropped down lower, trying to hide behind Wolf, my heart pounding.

Wolf hadn't moved, but he was silent now. His ears were still pulled back, his lips still open in a soundless snarl.

What were those dark stains on the front of the swamp hermit's grimy shirt?

Bloodstains?

A shiver of fear ran down my back.

Wolf stared straight ahead without blinking, without moving a muscle.

The swamp hermit disappeared behind the tall weeds. We couldn't see him, but we could still hear his footsteps crunching over dead leaves and fallen twigs.

I glanced over at Wolf. The big dog shook himself, as if shaking the swamp hermit from his mind. His tail wagged slowly. His body relaxed. He uttered soft whimpers, as if telling me how scared he had been.

"It's okay, boy," I said quietly, and rubbed the

soft fur on top of the dog's head. He stopped whimpering and licked my wrist.

"That man is creepy!" Will exclaimed, climbing slowly to his feet.

"He even scared the dog," I said, patting Wolf on the head again. "What do you think he had in the sack?"

"Probably someone's head!" Will said, his dark eyes wide with horror.

I laughed. But I stopped when I saw that Will wasn't joking. "Everyone says he's harmless," I said.

"He had blood all over the front of his shirt," Will said with a shudder. He scratched his short, dark hair nervously.

The sunlight faded quickly as clouds rolled over the sun. Long shadows crept over the bog. The stick Will had thrown had disappeared, sucked into the thick, murky water.

"Let's go home," I suggested.

"Yeah. Okay," Will agreed quickly.

I called Wolf, who was exploring in the tall weeds. Then we turned and started to make our way back along the twisting dirt path.

A soft breeze fluttered the trees, making the palm leaves scrape and clatter. Tall ferns shivered in the wind. The shadows grew deeper and darker.

I could hear Wolf behind us. I could hear his body brushing through low shrubs and weeds.

We were nearly back to where the trees ended and the flat grass leading to our back garden began. We were nearly out of the swamp when Will stopped suddenly.

I saw his mouth drop open in horror.

I turned to follow his gaze.

Then I uttered a shocked cry and covered my eyes to shut out the gruesome sight.

When I opened my eyes, the hideous pile of feathers and blood-covered flesh was still at my feet.

"Wh-what *is* it?" Will stammered.

It took me a long while to realize we were staring at a bird. A large heron.

It was hard to recognize because it had been torn apart.

Long, white feathers were scattered over the soft ground. The poor bird's chest had been torn wide open.

"The swamp hermit!" Will cried.

"Huh?" I cried. I turned away from the hideous sight and tried to force the image from my mind.

"That's why he had blood all over his shirt!" Will declared.

"But why would he rip a bird apart?" I asked weakly.

"Because . . . because he's a *monster!*" Will exclaimed.

"He's just a weird old guy who lives alone in the swamp," I said. "He didn't do this, Will. Some kind of animal did it. Look!" I pointed to the ground.

There were paw prints in the soft ground. All around the dead bird.

"They look like dog's paws," I said, thinking out loud.

"Dogs don't rip birds apart," Will replied quietly.

At that moment, Wolf came bounding up to us through the weeds. He came to a stop in front of the dead bird and started to sniff it.

"Get away from there, Wolf," I ordered. "Come on. Get away." I tugged him back, pulling him with both hands around his thick neck.

"Let's get home," Will said. "Let's get away from this thing. I'm going to have bad dreams. I really am."

I pulled Wolf with both hands. We stepped carefully around the dead heron and then hurried towards the swamp edge. Neither of us said a word. I guess we were both still picturing what we had seen.

As we reached the flat grass behind our houses, I said goodbye to Will. I watched him hurry to his house. Wolf scampered after him for part of the way. Then he turned and hurried back to me.

The late afternoon sun burned its way through

the clouds. I shielded my eyes from the sudden brightness, and saw my dad working in the deer pen behind the house.

"Hey, Dad—" I ran towards him over the grass.

He glanced up when I called to him. He was wearing denim cutoffs and a sleeveless yellow T-shirt. He had a baseball cap pulled down over his forehead. "What's up, Grady?"

"Will and I—we saw a dead heron," I told him breathlessly.

"Where? In the swamp?" he asked casually. He pulled off the cap, wiped his forehead with the back of his hand, and replaced the cap.

"Dad, it—it was torn apart!" I cried.

He didn't react. "That's part of life in the wild," he said, pulling up one of the deer's hooves to examine the bottom. "You know that, Grady. It can get quite violent out there. We've talked about survival of the fittest and stuff like that."

"No, Dad. This is different," I insisted. "The heron—it was ripped in two. I mean, as if someone had taken it, and—"

"Another bird, maybe," Dad said, concentrating on the deer hoof. "A larger bird of prey. It could have been—"

"We saw the swamp hermit," I interrupted. "He had blood all over his shirt. Then we saw paw prints in the ground. All around the dead bird."

"Grady, calm down," Dad said, letting go of the deer's leg. "If you go exploring in the swamp, you're going to see a lot of frightening-looking things. But don't let your imagination run away with you."

"Will said it was done by a monster!" I exclaimed.

Dad frowned and scratched his head through the cap. "I see your new friend has a good imagination, too," he said quietly.

That night, I was glad my parents agreed to let Wolf sleep in my room. I felt a lot safer with the big dog curled up on the rug beside my bed.

I hadn't been able to shake the ugly picture of the dead heron from my mind. I watched some TV until dinnertime. Then after dinner, I played a long chess game with Emily.

But no matter what I did, I kept seeing the white feathers scattered over the ground, the torn-apart bird lying crumpled on the path.

So now I felt a little comforted with Wolf sleeping in the room. "You'll protect me, won't you, boy?" I whispered from my bed.

He uttered a low snort. Light from the full moon spilled over him through the window. I saw that he was sleeping with his head resting on his two front paws.

Then I drifted into a dreamless sleep.

I don't know how long I slept.

I was awakened some time later by a horrifying crash.

I sat straight up with a startled gasp.

The crash had come from the living room, I realized.

Someone was breaking in!

Was it a burglar?

I climbed out of bed, my heart pounding, and crept to the door.

Another crash. A loud *thump*.

Footsteps.

"Who—who is it?" I cried. My voice came out in a choked whisper.

Keeping against the wall, I made my way slowly towards the living room. "Who's there?" I shouted.

Mum and Dad and Emily met me in the dark corridor. Even in the darkness I could see the fear and confusion on their faces.

I was the first to the living room. Pale yellow light from the full moon washed across the room. "Hey!" I called out.

Wolf leaped against the big front window. His shoulders made a loud *thud* against the glass.

"Wolf—stop!" I cried.

In the pale light, I saw what had caused the

loud crash. Wolf had knocked over the table and a lamp that had stood in front of the window.

"He—he's trying to get outside," I stammered.

I felt Dad's hand on the shoulder of my pyjama top. "What a mess he's made," he murmured.

"Wolf—stop!" I called again.

The big dog turned, breathing hard. His eyes glowed red in the moonlight through the window.

"Why is he so desperate to get out?" Emily demanded.

"We can't have him in the house if he does this every night," Mum said, her voice hoarse from sleep.

The big dog lowered his head and let out an excited growl. His tail stood straight up behind him.

"Open the front door. Let him out," Mum said. "Before he wrecks the whole house."

Dad hurried across the room and pulled open the door. Wolf didn't hesitate for a second. He bounded to the door and burst out.

I ran to the window to watch him. But the big dog disappeared around the side of the house, running towards the back garden.

"He's heading for the swamp," I said.

"He tried to break right through the window," Mum said.

Emily clicked on a lamp. "He's so strong, he

probably could have broken the window," she said quietly.

Dad closed the front door. He yawned. Then he turned his gaze on me. "You know what this means, don't you, Grady?"

I was still staring out at the full moon. "No. What?"

"Wolf will have to stay outdoors from now on," Dad said. He stooped and began picking up pieces of the broken lamp.

"But, Dad—" I started to protest.

"He's too big and too restless to stay in the house," Dad continued. He handed the lamp pieces to Emily. Then he pulled the table rightside up and returned it to its place in front of the window.

"Wolf didn't mean to break the lamp," I argued weakly.

"He'll break everything we have," Mum said quietly.

"He's just too big," Dad added. "He'll have to stay outside, Grady."

"Why did he want to get out so desperately?" Emily demanded.

"He's probably used to being outside," Dad told her. "He'll be happier out there," he said, turning to me.

"Yeah. Maybe," I replied glumly. I liked having Wolf sleeping beside me in my bedroom. But I knew there was no way I could convince my parents to give the dog a second chance. Their minds were made up.

And at least they were letting me keep Wolf.

I pulled the vacuum cleaner out of the cupboard and plugged it in. Dad took the nozzle and began vacuuming up the tiny pieces of glass from the carpet.

That crazy dog, I thought, shaking my head unhappily. What is his *problem*, anyway?

When Dad finished, I carried the vacuum cleaner back to the cupboard.

"Now maybe we can all sleep in peace," Mum said, yawning.

She was wrong.

17

I heard the frightening howls again a short while later.

At first I thought I was dreaming them.

But when I opened my eyes and gazed around my dark bedroom, the howls continued. Still half asleep, I gripped the covers with both hands and pulled them up to my chin.

The howls sounded so close, as if they were right outside my window. They didn't seem like the cries of an animal. They were too angry, too deliberate.

Too human.

Stop trying to frighten yourself, I thought. It's a wolf. It has to be some kind of swamp wolf.

In the back of my mind, I knew it might be Wolf making those frightening sounds. But I kept pushing the thought away.

Why would the dog howl like that?

Dogs bark. They don't howl unless they're very sad or upset.

I shut my eyes, wishing the frightening wails away.

Suddenly, they stopped. Silence.

Then I heard rapid thumps on the ground. Footsteps.

Some kind of a struggle.

I heard a short, terrifying cry. It cut off almost as soon as it began.

It's right at the back of the house, I realized.

Wide awake now, I jumped out of bed, dragging the covers with me. I stumbled to the bedroom window and grabbed the windowsill.

The full moon had risen high in the night sky. The back garden stretched out silvery in the moonlight, the dewy grass shimmering in the bright light.

Pressing my forehead against the windowpane, I peered out towards the dark swamp. I uttered a near-silent gasp when I saw the shadowy creature running towards the trees.

A large creature, running on all fours.

It was only a black outline fading into the darkness. But I could see how big it was, and I could see how fast it was running.

And I heard its howls. Triumphant howls, I thought.

Is it Wolf? I wondered. I peered out of the window without moving, even though the darkness had swallowed the creature up. I could see only the outline of distant trees.

71

But I could still hear the howls rising and falling on the heavy night air.

Is it Wolf?

It can't be Wolf—can it?

I lowered my gaze. My breath caught in my throat. I saw something. In the middle of the back garden. A few metres from the deer pen.

At first I thought it was a pile of rags.

My hands trembled as I pulled open my window.

I had to get a better look. I had to see what that was in the back garden.

I pulled up my pyjama bottoms. Then, gripping the window-sill, I lowered myself out of the window on to the grass.

The wet grass felt cold under my bare feet. I turned to the deer pen. The six swamp deer were standing tensely huddled together against the house. Their dark eyes followed me as I began to creep across the grass.

What *is* that thing? I wondered, staring into the silvery light.

Is it just a pile of old rags?

No.

What *is* it?

My bare feet felt cold and wet as I made my way slowly across the dew-covered grass. The night air was heavy and still, still as death.

When I came close enough to see what was lying in a heap on the grass, I uttered a faint cry and started to retch.

I pressed a hand against my mouth and swallowed hard.

I realized I was staring down at a dead rabbit. Its small, black eyes were frozen open in terror. One of its ears had been pulled off.

The rabbit had been ripped open, nearly torn in half.

I forced myself to look away.

My stomach still heaving, I hurried back over the wet grass to my open window and scrambled back in.

As I struggled to pull the window shut, the howls rang out again, rising triumphantly from the nearby swamp.

After breakfast the next morning, I led Dad out
to the back garden to show him the murdered
rabbit. It was a bright, hot day, and a red sun
climbed a pale, clear sky.

As soon as we stepped off the back patio, Wolf
appeared from around the side of the house. His
tail began wagging furiously. He came running
excitedly to greet me, as if he hadn't seen me in
years, leaping on to my chest, nearly knocking
me over.

"Down, Wolf! Down!" I cried, laughing as the
dog stretched to lick my face.

"Your dog is a killer," a voice said behind me. I
turned to see that Emily had followed us. She
was wearing a red T-shirt over white tennis
shorts. She had her arms crossed in front of her,
and she was glaring disapprovingly at Wolf.
"Look what he did to that poor bunny rabbit,"
she said, shaking her head.

"Whoa. Hold on," I replied, patting Wolf's
grey fur. "Who said Wolf did this?"

"Who else would have done it?" demanded
Emily. "He's a killer."

"Oh, yeah? Look how gentle he is," I insisted. I
put my wrist in Wolf's mouth. He clamped down
gently on it, being careful not to hurt me.

"Wolf *may* be a bit of a hunter," Dad said
thoughtfully. He had been staring down at the

rabbit, but now he turned his gaze to the deer pen.

Huddled together at one end of the pen, the deer were all staring warily at Wolf. They had their heads lowered cautiously as they followed the dog's every move.

"I'm glad they're safe inside that pen," Dad said softly.

"Dad, you have to get rid of this dog," Emily said shrilly.

"No chance!" I cried. I turned angrily to my sister. "You have no proof that Wolf did anything wrong!" I shouted. "No proof at all!"

"You have no proof that he *didn't* do it!" Emily replied nastily.

"Of *course* he didn't!" I cried, feeling myself lose control. "Didn't you hear the howls last night? Didn't you hear those frightening howls? It wasn't a *dog* howling like that. Dogs don't howl like that!"

"Then what was it?" Emily demanded.

"I heard them, too," Dad said, stepping between us. "They sounded like wolf howls. Or maybe a coyote."

"See?" I told Emily.

"But I'd be very surprised to find a wolf or coyote in *this* area," Dad continued, gazing out towards the swamp.

Emily still had her arms crossed tightly over her chest. She gazed down at Wolf and shuddered. "He's dangerous, Dad. You really have to get rid of him."

Dad walked over and patted Wolf's head. He scratched Wolf under the chin. Wolf licked Dad's hand.

"Let's just be careful with him," Dad said. "He seems very gentle. But we don't really know anything about him—do we? So let's be very careful, okay?"

"I'm going to be careful," Emily replied, narrowing her eyes at Wolf. "I'm going to stay as far away from that *monster* as I can." She turned and stormed back to the house.

Dad made his way to the shed to get a shovel and box to carry away the dead rabbit.

I dropped to my knees and hugged Wolf's broad neck. "You aren't a monster, are you, boy?" I asked. "Emily is crazy, isn't she? You're not a monster. That wasn't you I saw running towards the swamp last night, was it?"

Wolf raised his deep blue eyes to mine. He stared hard at me.

He seemed to be trying to tell me something.

But I had no idea what it could be.

That night I didn't hear the howls.

I woke up in the middle of the night and stared out of the window. Wolf was gone, probably exploring the swamp. In the morning, I knew he'd come running back to greet me as if I were a long lost friend.

The next morning Will showed up just as I was giving Wolf his breakfast, a big bowl of crunchy, dry dog food. "Hey, what's up?" Will asked, his usual greeting.

"Nothing much," I said. I rolled up the top of the big bag of dog food and dragged it back into the kitchen. Wolf stood over his bowl, his head lowered, chewing noisily away.

I pushed open the screen door and returned to Will. He was wearing a dark blue muscle shirt and black Lycra bike shorts. He had a green-and-yellow Forest Service cap pulled down over his dark hair.

"Want to go exploring?" he asked in his

hoarse voice, watching Wolf hungrily gobble up his breakfast. "You know. In the swamp?"

"Yeah. Okay," I said. I called inside to tell my parents where I was going. Then I followed Will across the back lawn towards the swamp.

Wolf came scampering after us. He'd run past us, then let us catch up. Then he'd run in crazy zigzags in front of us, behind us, romping happily under the hot morning sun.

"Did you hear about Mr Warner?" Will asked. He stopped to pick up a long blade of grass and put it between his teeth.

"Who?"

"Ed Warner," Will replied. "I suppose you haven't met the Warners yet. They live in the very last house." He turned and pointed behind us to the last white house at the end of the row of white houses.

"What about him?" I asked, nearly tripping over Wolf, who had come rumbling past my feet.

"He's missing," Will replied, chewing on the grass blade. "He didn't come home last night."

"Huh? From where?" I asked, turning to stare at the Warners' house. Heat waves shimmered up from the grass, making the house appear to bend and quiver.

"From the swamp," Will replied darkly. "Mrs Warner called my mum this morning. She said Mr Warner went hunting yesterday afternoon. He likes to hunt wild turkeys. He took me with him a couple of times. He's really good at chasing them down. When he kills one, he hangs its feet up on his shed wall."

"He does?" I cried. It sounded pretty disgusting to me.

"Yeah. You know. Like a trophy," Will continued. "Anyway, he was hunting wild turkeys in the swamp yesterday afternoon, and he hasn't come home."

"Strange," I said, watching Wolf stop at the edge of the trees. "Maybe he got lost."

"No chance," Will insisted, shaking his head. "Not Mr Warner. He's lived here a long time. He was the first one to move here. Mr Warner wouldn't get lost."

"Then maybe the werewolf got him!" called a strange voice behind us.

Startled, we both spun around to see a girl about our age. She had rust-coloured red hair tied in a ponytail on one side. She had cat-like green eyes, and a short stub of a nose, and freckles all over her face. She was wearing faded red denim jeans and a T-shirt with a grinning green alligator on the front.

"Cassie, what are *you* doing here?" Will demanded.

"Following you," she replied, making a face at him. She turned to me. "You're the new kid, Grady, right? Will told me about you."

"Hi," I said awkwardly. "He told me a girl lived in the neighbourhood. But he didn't tell me much about you."

"What is there to tell?" Will teased.

"I'm Cassie O'Rourke," she said. She shot up her hand and pulled the blade of grass from Will's mouth.

"Hey!" He playfully tried to whack her, but missed.

"What did you say about a werewolf?" I asked.

"Don't start with that stuff again," Will grumbled to Cassie. "It's so stupid."

"You're just afraid," Cassie accused.

"No, I'm not. It's too stupid," Will insisted.

We stepped into the shade of the trees at the swamp edge. A funnel cloud of white gnats whirred crazily in a shaft of light between the trees.

"There's a werewolf in the swamp," Cassie said, lowering her voice as we ducked past the gnats and moved deeper into the shade.

"And I'm going to flap my wings and fly to Mars," Will said sarcastically.

"Shut up, Will," Cassie snapped. "Grady doesn't think it's stupid—do you?"

I shrugged. "I don't know," I said. "I don't think I believe in werewolves."

Will laughed. "Cassie believes in the Easter Bunny, too," he said.

Cassie socked him hard in the chest.

"Hey!" Will cried out angrily as he staggered back. "What's your problem?"

"Mosquito," she said, pointing. "A big one. I got him."

Scowling, Will glanced down. "I can't see any mosquito. Give me a break, Cassie."

We made our way along the winding path. It

had rained the day before. The ground was marshier than usual. We kept slipping in the soft mud.

"Do you hear the howling sounds at night?" I asked Cassie.

"That's the werewolf," she replied softly. Her green cat-eyes burned into mine. "I'm not joking, Grady. I'm serious. Those howls aren't human. Those howls come from a werewolf who has just killed."

Will sniggered. "You've got a good imagination, Cassie. I suppose you watch a lot of scary films on TV, huh?"

"Real life is scarier than the films," she said, lowering her voice to a whisper.

"Ooh, stop. You're making me shake all over!" Will exclaimed sarcastically.

She didn't reply. She was still staring at me as we walked. "You believe me, don't you?"

"I don't know," I said.

The bog came into view. The air became heavier, wetter. The tall weeds on the other side stood straight up. The bog gurgled quietly. Two big flies danced over the dark green surface.

"There's no such thing as werewolves, Cassie," Will muttered, searching for something to throw into the bog. He grinned at her. "Unless maybe *you're* one!"

She rolled her eyes. "Very funny." She made

biting motions with her teeth as if she were going to bite him.

I heard a rustling sound across the oval-shaped bog. The tall weeds suddenly parted, and Wolf appeared at the edge of the water.

"What does the werewolf look like?" Will asked sarcastically. "Does it have red hair and freckles?"

Cassie didn't reply.

I turned to see a look of terror freeze on her face. Her green eyes grew wide, and her freckles seemed to fade. "The-there's the *werewolf!*" she stammered in a choked whisper. She pointed.

Feeling a chill of fear, I turned to see where she was pointing.

To my horror, she was pointing right at Wolf!

21

"No!" I started to protest.

But then I saw that I had misunderstood. Cassie wasn't pointing at Wolf. She was pointing to the figure moving through the tall weeds behind the dog.

The swamp hermit!

I saw him walking quickly behind the weeds, his shoulders bent, his mangy head bobbing with each step.

As he moved into a small break in the weeds, I could see why he was leaning forward. He carried something over one shoulder. A bag of some sort.

Wolf started to growl.

The hermit stopped walking.

It wasn't a bag slung over his shoulder, I saw. It was a turkey. A wild turkey.

A chilling thought burst into my mind. Had he taken it from Mr Warner?

Was Cassie right about the swamp hermit?

Was he a werewolf? Had he done something horrible to Mr Warner and claimed the wild turkey as his prize?

I tried to dismiss these horrible thoughts. They were crazy. Impossible.

But Cassie looked so frightened, staring across the gurgling green bog at the wild-eyed hermit. And the howls at night, the howls had been so frightening, so human.

And the dead animals I'd seen, torn so brutally apart, as if . . . as if by a werewolf!

Wolf uttered another warning growl. He stared at the hermit, his tail standing stiffly behind him, his fur rising up on his back.

The hermit moved quickly. I saw his dark eyes flash just before he disappeared behind the weeds.

"It's him!" Cassie cried, still pointing. "It's the werewolf!"

"Cassie—*shut up*!" Will warned. "He'll *hear* you!"

I swallowed hard, frozen in place by my fear. I saw the weeds tremble across the bog. I heard rustling sounds growing closer.

"Run!" Will cried, his hoarse voice shrill and frightened. "Come on—run!"

Too late.

The swamp hermit burst out of the weeds right behind us. "I'm the werewolf!" he shrieked. His eyes were wild, excited. His face, surrounded by

85

his long, tangled hair, was bright red. "I'm the werewolf!"

He *had* heard Cassie!

Laughing at the top of his lungs, he tossed up both hands, then began to swing the turkey in a wide circle over his head. "I'm the werewolf!" he cried.

Cassie, Will, and I all cried out at the same time.

Then we started to run.

Out of the corner of my eye, I could see Wolf. He hadn't moved from his spot across the bog. But now, as I started to run, he came bounding towards us, barking excitedly.

"I'm the werewolf!" the hermit shrieked. He howled with laughter, still swinging the turkey as he chased after us.

"Leave us alone!" Cassie cried, running beside Will a few steps ahead of me. "Do you *hear* me? Leave us alone!"

Her pleas made the hermit howl again.

My shoes slipped in the muddy ground.

I turned back. He was gaining on me. Right behind me.

Gasping for breath, I struggled to run faster. Sharp vines and heavy leaves slapped at my face and arms as I plunged forward.

It was all a blur now. A blur of light and shade, trees and vines, tall weeds and sharp brambles.

"I'm the werewolf! I'm the werewolf!"

The crazed hermit's high-pitched wails of laughter echoed through the swamp.

Keep going, Grady, I urged myself. Keep going.

Then, with a terrified cry, I felt my feet slide out from under me.

I fell face forward into the mud, landing hard on my hands and knees.

He's got me, I realized.

The werewolf has got me.

I tried frantically to scramble up from the mud. But I slipped again and tumbled forward with a *splat*.

He's got me now, I thought.

The werewolf has got me now. I cannot escape.

My muscles all froze in panic. I struggled to crawl away.

I turned back, expecting the hermit to grab me.

But he had stopped several metres away. The turkey dangled to the ground as he stared down at me, a strange grin on his weathered face.

Where was Wolf? I wondered.

Wolf had been growling furiously at the swamp hermit. Why hadn't Wolf attacked?

"Help! Will! Cassie!" I called desperately.

Silence.

They were gone. They were both probably out of the swamp by now, running for home.

I was alone. Alone to face the hermit.

I stumbled to my feet, my eyes locked on his. Why was he grinning at me like that?

"Go on. Go," he murmured, gesturing with his free hand. "Just teasing you."

"What?" My voice came out tiny and frightened.

"Go on. I'm not going to bite you," he said. His grin faded. The light seemed to dim in his shiny black eyes.

Wolf appeared behind him. The dog gazed up at the hermit, then lowered his eyes to the dead turkey. He barked once, a shrill *yip*. But I could see that Wolf had relaxed. He had no intention of attacking the hermit.

"This dog yours?" the hermit asked, eyeing Wolf warily.

"Yeah," I replied, still breathing hard. "I . . . found him."

"Watch out for him," the hermit said sharply. Then he turned and, hoisting the large bird on his shoulder, headed back into the weeds.

"W-watch out for him?" I stammered. "What do you mean?"

But the hermit didn't reply. I could hear him brushing the tall weeds away as he disappeared back into the swamp.

"What do you mean?" I called after him.

But he was gone. The swamp was silent now except for the chirping and clicking of insects and the dry sound of palm leaves brushing against each other.

I stared straight ahead at the tall weeds. I think I expected the swamp hermit to return, to burst back into view, to attack again.

Two white moths fluttered together over the weeds. Nothing else moved.

He was teasing us, he had said.

That's all it was, just teasing.

I swallowed hard. Then I forced myself to breathe normally again.

After a while, I lowered my gaze to Wolf. The dog was busily sniffing the ground where the hermit had stood.

"Wolf—why didn't you protect me?" I scolded.

The dog glanced up, then returned to his sniffing.

"Hey, dog—are you a big coward?" I asked, brushing at the wet dirt on the knees of my jeans. "Is that your problem? You sound really tough, but you're actually a big chicken?"

Wolf ignored me.

I turned and headed home, thinking about the hermit's warning. As I made my way along the narrow path, I could hear Wolf running through the weeds and tall grass, following close behind.

"*Watch out for him*," the hermit had said.

Was he teasing about that, too? Was he just trying to scare me?

The strange man saw that Will, Cassie, and I

were afraid of him. So he decided to have some fun with us.

That's all it was, I decided.

He heard Cassie call him a werewolf. So he decided to give us a real scare.

As I walked along the marshy ground under the shade of the tilted palm trees, my mind spun with thoughts about Cassie and Will and Wolf and werewolves.

I didn't see the snake until I stepped on it.

I glanced down in time to see its bright green head shoot forwards.

I felt a sharp stab of pain as its fangs dug into my ankle.

The pain jolted up my leg.

I uttered a choked gasp before I crumpled to the ground.

I hit the ground and curled into a tight ball as the pain throbbed through my body.

Red dots formed in my eyes. The dots grew larger and larger until I saw only red. The colour shimmered in rhythm to the throbbing pain.

Through the curtain of red, I saw the snake slither into the bushes.

I grabbed my ankle, trying to force the pain down.

Slowly, the red faded, then vanished, leaving only the pain.

My hand suddenly felt wet.

Blood?

I glanced down to see Wolf licking my hand. Fierce licking, as if trying to cure me, trying to make everything okay again.

Despite the pain, I laughed. "It's okay, boy," I said. "I'm okay."

He kept licking my hand until I climbed to my feet. I felt a little dizzy. My legs were shaky.

I tried putting weight on the foot that had been bitten.

It felt a little better.

I took a step, limping. Then another.

"Let's go, Wolf," I said. He gazed up at me sympathetically.

I knew I had to get home quickly. If the snake was poisonous, I was in big trouble. I had no way of knowing how much time I had before the venom would paralyse me completely—or worse.

Wolf stayed by my side as I limped over the soft ground towards home. I was gasping for breath. My chest felt tight. The ground swayed beneath me.

Was it because of the snake venom? Or was it just because I was so frightened?

Pain shot up my side with every step I took.

But I kept pulling myself along, talking to Wolf all the while, ignoring the throbbing ache of my ankle.

"We're almost there, Wolf," I said, panting loudly. "Almost there, boy."

The dog sensed that something was seriously wrong. He stayed by my side instead of running his usual zigzag patterns in front of me and behind me.

The end of the trees came into view. I could see bright sunlight just beyond the swamp.

"Hey—" a voice called to me. I saw Will and

Cassie waiting for me on the flat grass.

They began running towards me. "Are you okay?" Cassie called.

"No. I . . . I've been *bitten*!" I managed to choke out. "Please—go and get my dad!"

They both took off, running full speed to my house. I dropped down on the grass, spreading my legs straight out, and waited.

I tried to stay calm, but it was impossible.

Was the snake poisonous? Was the venom heading straight for my heart? Was I about to die any second?

I reached down with both hands and carefully, carefully, pulled off my mud-covered trainer. Then, moving it a tiny bit at a time, I lowered my white sock down the ankle and off my foot.

The ankle was a little swollen. The skin was red except for a white, puckered spot around the bite. Inside that spot, I saw two small puncture marks, bright red droplets of blood oozing from each hole.

When I raised my eyes from the wound, I saw my dad, dressed in brown shorts and a white T-shirt, hurrying along the flat grass towards me, followed closely by Will and Cassie.

"What happened?" I heard my dad ask them. "What happened to Grady?"

"He was bitten by a werewolf!" I heard Cassie reply.

*

"Keep the ice pack on it," Dad instructed. "The swelling will go down."

I groaned and held the ice pack against my ankle.

Mum tsk-tsked from the kitchen table. She had a newspaper spread out in front of her. I couldn't tell if she was tsk-tsking over me or over the day's news.

Outside the screen door I could see Wolf, on his side on the grass just beyond the back patio, sound asleep. Emily was in the front room, watching some soap opera on TV.

"How does it feel?" Mum asked.

"A lot better," I told her. "I think I was mainly scared."

"Green snakes aren't poisonous," Dad reminded me for the tenth time. "But I took every precaution, just in case. We'll wrap it up really well when you've finished putting ice on it."

"What was all that talk about werewolves?" Mum asked.

"Cassie has werewolves on the brain," I said. "She thinks the swamp hermit is a werewolf."

"She seems like a sweet girl," Mum said quietly. "I had a nice talk with her while your father was taking care of your bite. You're lucky, Grady, to find two kids your age out here on the edge of a swamp."

"Yeah, I suppose so," I replied, shifting the ice

pack on the ankle. "But she was driving Will and me nuts with all her werewolf talk."

Dad was washing his hands in the kitchen sink. He dried them on a dish towel, then turned to me. "That old swamp hermit is supposed to be harmless," he said. "At least, that's what everyone says."

"Well, he gave us a real scare," I told him. 'He chased us through the swamp, shouting, "I'm the werewolf!"'

"Weird," Dad replied thoughtfully. He tossed the dish towel on to the work top.

"You should stay away from him," Mum said, looking up from the newspaper.

"Do you believe in werewolves?" I asked.

Dad sniggered. "Your mum and I are scientists, Grady. We're not supposed to believe in supernatural things like werewolves."

"Your father is a werewolf," Mum joked. "I have to shave his back every morning so he'll look human."

"Ha-ha," I said sarcastically. "I'm serious. I mean, haven't you heard the weird howls at night?"

"Lots of creatures howl," Mum replied. "I'll bet *you* howled when that snake bit your ankle!"

"Can't you be serious?" I cried shrilly. "You know, the howls didn't start until it was a full moon."

"I remember. The howls didn't start until that

dog turned up!" Emily called from the front room.

"Emily, give me a break!" I shouted.

"Your dog is a werewolf!" Emily called.

"Enough werewolf talk," Mum muttered. "Look. I've got hair growing on my palms!" She held up her hands.

"That's just ink off the newspaper," Dad said. He turned to me. "See? There's a scientific explanation for everything."

"I really would like to be taken seriously," I said through clenched teeth.

"Well . . ." Dad glanced outside. Wolf had rolled on to his back and was sleeping with all four legs up in the air. "The moon will look full for only two more nights," Dad told me. "Tonight and tomorrow night. If the howls stop after tomorrow night, we'll know it was a werewolf, howling at the full moon."

Dad chuckled. He thought it was all a big joke.

We had no idea that something was about to happen that night that might change his opinion about werewolves—forever.

Will and Cassie came over after dinner. Mum and Dad were still loading dishes into the dishwasher and cleaning up. Emily had hurried into town to go to the only film on.

I was walking around fairly well. The ankle barely hurt at all. Dad's a pretty good doctor, I suppose.

The three of us settled in the front room, and we instantly got into an argument about werewolves.

Cassie insisted that the swamp hermit wasn't joking, that he really was a werewolf.

Will told her she was a complete idiot. "He only chased us because he heard you call him a werewolf," he told Cassie angrily.

"Why do you think he lives by himself deep in the swamp?" Cassie demanded of Will. "Because he knows what happens to him when the moon is full, and he doesn't want anyone else to know!"

"Then why did he scream to us that he was a werewolf this afternoon?" Will asked impatiently. "Because he was just joking, that's why."

"Come on, guys. Let's change the subject," I said. "My parents are both scientists, and they say there's no proof that werewolves exist."

"That's what scientists always say," Cassie insisted.

"They're right," Will said. "There are no werewolves except in films. You're a real idiot, Cassie."

"*You're* an idiot!" Cassie shouted back.

I could see they'd had fights like this before. "Let's play a game or something," I suggested. "Want to play some Nintendo? It's in my room."

"Mr Warner still hasn't turned up," Cassie told Will, ignoring me. She tugged at her red ponytail, then tossed it behind her head. "You know why? Because he was murdered by the werewolf!"

"Don't be stupid," Will said. "How do *you* know?"

"Maybe *you're* the werewolf!" I told Cassie.

Will laughed. "Yeah. That's why you're such an expert, Cassie."

"Oh, shut up," Cassie grumbled. "You look more like a werewolf than me, Will!"

"You look like a *vampire*!" he told her.

"Well, you look like King Kong!" she cried.

99

"What are you kids talking about?" Mum interrupted, poking her head into the room.

"Just talking about films and things," I replied quickly.

I couldn't get to sleep that night. I kept rolling on to one side, then the other. I couldn't get comfortable.

I kept listening for the howls.

A strong wind had come up from the Gulf. I could hear it rushing past our small house. It rattled the wire mesh of the deer pen behind the house. It made a constant *ssshhhhh* sound, and I strained to hear the familiar howls.

I had just about drifted off to sleep when the howls began.

Instantly alert, I jumped to my feet. My left ankle ached as I stepped down on it.

Another howl. Far off. Barely carrying over the steady rush of the wind.

I limped to my bedroom window. My ankle had stiffened up a bit while I was lying in bed. I pressed my face against the glass and peered out.

The full moon, grey as a skull, hovered low in the charcoal sky. The dewy grass gleamed under its blanket of pale light.

A burst of wind rattled my window.

Startled, I pulled back. And listened.

Another howl. Closer.

This one sent a cold shudder down my back.

It sounded really close. Or was the wind carrying it from the swamp?

I squinted out of the window. Swirls of wind made the grass sway from one side to the other. The ground appeared to be spinning, glowing in the pale moonlight as it twirled.

Another howl. Even closer.

I couldn't see anything. I *had* to know who or what was making that terrifying sound.

I pulled my jeans on over my pyjama bottoms. Struggling in the dark, I managed to slide my feet into a pair of flip-flops.

I started walking out of my room, but stopped short when I heard a banging. A loud crash. A pounding. A harsh *thud*.

Right outside.

Right outside my house.

My heart pounding, I ran through the dark corridor.

My ankle ached, but I ignored it.

I hurried through the kitchen, unlocked the back door, and pulled it open. A strong gust of wind pushed me back as I opened the screen door.

The wind was hot and wet. Another strong gust pushed me back.

The wind is trying to keep me inside, I thought. Trying to keep me from solving the mystery of the terrifying howls.

I lowered my head against the driving gusts and leapt down off the patio.

"Ow!" I cried out as pain shot up my leg.

Waiting for my eyes to adjust to the dim light, I listened hard.

No howls now. Just the shrill, steady rush of wind, pushing, pushing me back against the house.

The back garden glowed in the moonlight. Everything was silver and grey.

And silent.

I searched the back garden, my eyes sweeping slowly across the shifting grass. Empty.

But what had caused all the commotion I'd heard in my room? The banging? The loud *thuds*? The rattling sounds?

Why had the howls stopped when I came outside?

What a mystery, I thought. What a strange mystery.

The wind swirled around me. My face was dripping wet from the heavy dampness of the air.

Feeling defeated, I turned back towards the house.

And uttered a shocked cry when I saw that the werewolf had murdered again.

I took a step through the swirling wind towards the deer pen.

"Dad!" I called. But my voice came out a hushed whisper. "Dad!" I tried to shout, but my throat was too dry and choked with fear.

Staring straight ahead, I took another step. I could see it all clearly now. A scene of death. Pale light and shadows. The only sounds were the pounding of my heart, the swell of the wind, and the rattling of the wire mesh of the pen.

I took another step closer. "Dad? Dad?" I cried without thinking, without hearing myself, knowing he couldn't hear.

But I wanted him to be there. I wanted *someone* to be there with me. I didn't want to be all alone out there in the back garden.

I didn't want to be staring at the hole that had been ripped from the side of the pen. I didn't want to see the murdered deer lying so pitifully on its side.

The five remaining deer huddled together at the other end of the pen. Their eyes were on me. Frightened eyes.

The wind swept around me, hot and wet. But I felt cold all over. A cold shudder of terror ran down my body. I swallowed hard. Once. Twice. Trying to choke down the heavy lump in my throat.

Then, before I even realized what I was doing, I began running to the house, screaming, "Dad! Mum! Dad! Mum!" at the top of my lungs.

My cries rose on the gusting wind like the terrifying howls I'd heard just a few moments before.

His pyjama shirt flapping over the jeans he had pulled on, Dad dragged the dead deer to the back of the yard. Then, as I watched from the kitchen window, he patched the deer pen with a large sheet of hardboard.

As he tried to return to the house, the strong winds nearly blew the screen door off its hinges. Dad jerked the door shut, then locked it.

His face was dripping with perspiration. He had mud down the side of one pyjama sleeve.

Mum poured him a glass of water from the sink, and he drank it down without taking a breath. Then he wiped the sweat from his forehead with a tea towel.

"I'm afraid your dog is a killer," he said softly

to me. He tossed the towel back on to the counter.

"It wasn't Wolf!" I cried. "It wasn't!"

Dad didn't reply. He took a deep breath, then let it out slowly. Mum and Emily watched silently from in front of the sink.

"What makes you think it was Wolf?" I demanded.

"I saw the prints on the ground," he replied, frowning. "Paw prints."

"It wasn't Wolf," I insisted.

"I'm going to have to take him to the pound in the morning," Dad said. "The one over in the next county."

"But they'll kill him," I cried.

"The dog is a killer," Dad insisted softly. "I know how you feel, Grady. I know. But the dog is a killer."

"It wasn't Wolf," I cried. "Dad, I know it wasn't Wolf. I heard the howls, Dad. It was a werewolf."

"Grady, please—" he started wearily.

Then the words just burst out of me. I lost all control of them. They just poured out in a flood. "It was a werewolf, Dad. There's a werewolf in the swamp. Cassie is right. It wasn't a dog, and it wasn't a wolf. It's a werewolf who's been killing animals, who killed your deer."

"Grady, stop—" Dad pleaded impatiently.

But I couldn't stop. "I know I'm right, Dad," I cried in a shrill voice that didn't sound like me.

"It's been a full moon this week, right? And that's when the howls began. It's a werewolf, Dad. The swamp hermit. That crazy man who lives in the shack in the swamp. He's a werewolf. He told us he is. He chased us and he told us he's a werewolf. *He* did it, Dad. Not Wolf. *He* killed the deer tonight. I heard him howling outside, and then—then—"

My voice caught in my throat. I started to choke.

Dad filled the glass with water and handed it to me. I gulped it down thirstily.

He put a hand on my shoulder. "Grady, let's talk about it in the morning, okay? We're both too tired to think straight now. What do you say?"

"It wasn't Wolf!" I cried stubbornly. "I know it wasn't."

"In the morning," Dad repeated, his hand still on my shoulder. He held it there to comfort me, to steady me.

I felt shaky. I was panting. My heart pounded.

"Yeah. Okay," I agreed finally. "In the morning."

I made my way slowly to my room, but I knew I wouldn't sleep.

The next morning, Dad was gone when I got up. "He went to the builder's yard," Mum told me, "to get wire mesh to repair the pen."

I yawned and stretched. I had fallen into a restless sleep at about two-thirty. But I still felt tired and nervous.

"Is Wolf out there?" I asked anxiously. I ran to the kitchen window before she could reply.

I could see Wolf at the top of the driveway. He had a blue rubber ball between his front paws, and he was chewing at it furiously.

"Bet he's hungry for breakfast," I muttered.

I heard the crunch of gravel, and Dad's car pulled up the drive. The boot was opened partway, a roll of wire mesh bulging inside.

"Morning," Dad said as he came into the kitchen. His expression was grim.

"Are you going to take Wolf?" I demanded immediately. My eyes were on the dog, chewing the rubber ball outside. He looked so cute.

"People in town are upset," Dad replied, pouring himself a cup of coffee from the coffee-maker. "A lot of animals have been killed this week. And a man who lives down the road, Ed Warner, has disappeared in the swamp. People are very worried. They've heard the howls, too."

"Are you taking Wolf away?" I repeated shrilly, my voice trembling.

Dad nodded. His expression remained grim. He took a long sip of coffee. "Go and look at the paw prints outside the pen, Grady," he said, locking his eyes on mine. "Go ahead. Take a look."

"I don't care about prints," I moaned. "I just know—"

"I can't take any more chances," Dad said.

"I don't care! He's my dog!" I screamed.

"Grady—" Dad put down the cup and started towards me.

But I burst past him and ran to the door. Pushing open the screen door, I leapt off the doorstep.

Wolf stood up as soon as he saw me. His tail started to wag. Leaving the blue rubber ball behind, he began loping towards me eagerly.

Dad was right behind me. "I'm going to take the dog away now, Grady," he said. "Do you want to come along?"

"No!" I cried.

"I have no choice," Dad said, his voice just above a whisper. He stepped forward and reached for Wolf.

"No!" I shouted. "No! Run, Wolf! Run!"

I gave the dog a shove. Wolf turned to me uncertainly.

"Run!" I screamed. "Run! Run!"

I gave Wolf another hard shove. "Run! Run, boy! Go!"

Dad had his hands around Wolf's shoulders, but he didn't have a good grip.

Wolf broke free and started to run towards the swamp.

"Hey—!" Dad called angrily. He chased Wolf to the end of the back garden. But the big dog was too fast for him.

I stood behind the house, breathing hard, and watched Wolf until he disappeared into the low trees at the edge of the swamp.

Dad turned back towards me, an angry expression on his face. "That was stupid, Grady," he muttered.

I didn't say anything.

"Wolf will come back later," Dad said. "When he does, I'll have to take him away."

"But, Dad—" I started.

"No more discussion," he said sternly. "As

soon as the dog returns, I'm taking him to the pound."

"You *can't!*" I screamed.

"The dog is a killer, Grady. I have no choice." Dad headed towards the car. "Come and help me unload this wire mesh. I'll need your help getting the pen patched up."

I gazed towards the swamp as I followed Dad to the car. *Don't come back, Wolf*, I pleaded silently.

Please don't come back.

All day long, I watched the swamp. I felt nervous, shaky. I had no appetite at all. After I helped Dad repair the deer pen, I stayed in my room. I tried to read a book, but the words were just a blur.

By evening, Wolf hadn't returned.

You're safe, Wolf! I thought. *At least for today.*

My whole family was tense. At dinner, we hardly spoke. Emily talked about the film she had seen the night before, but no one joined in with any comments.

I went to bed early. I was really tired. From stress, I suppose. And from being up most of the night before.

My room was darker than usual. It was the last night of the full moon, but heavy blankets of clouds covered the moonlight.

I settled my head on to my pillow and tried to

get to sleep. But I kept thinking about Wolf.

The howls started a short while later.

I crept out of bed and hurried to the window. I squinted out into the darkness. Heavy, black clouds still covered the moon. The air was still. Nothing moved.

I heard a low growl, and Wolf came into focus.

He was standing stiffly in the middle of the back garden, his head tilted up to the sky, uttering low growls. As I stared out of the window at him, the big dog began to pace, back and forth from one side of the garden to the other.

He's pacing like a caged animal, I thought. Pacing and growling, as if something is really troubling him.

Or *scaring* him.

As he paced, he kept raising his head towards the full moon behind the clouds and growling.

What is going on? I wondered. I had to find out.

I got dressed quickly in the darkness, pulling on the jeans and T-shirt I had worn all day.

I fumbled into my trainers. At first I had the left one on the right foot. It was so dark in my room without the moonlight pouring in!

As soon as my shoelaces were tied, I hurried back to the window. Wolf was leaving the back garden, I saw. He was lumbering slowly in the direction of the swamp.

111

I'm going to follow Wolf, I decided. I'm going to prove once and for all that he isn't a killer—or a werewolf.

I was afraid my parents might hear me if I went to the kitchen door. So I crawled out of my window.

The grass was wet from a heavy dew. The air was wet, too, and nearly as hot as during the day. My trainers squeaked and slid on the damp grass as I hurried to follow Wolf.

I stopped at the end of the back garden. I'd lost him.

I could still hear him somewhere up ahead. I could hear the soft *thud* of his paws on the marshy ground.

But it was too dark to see him.

I followed the sound of his footsteps, gazing up at the shifting, shadowy clouds.

I was almost at the swamp when I heard footsteps behind me.

With a gasp of fright, I stopped and listened hard.

Yes. Footsteps.

Moving rapidly towards me.

27

"Hey!"

I let out a choked cry and spun around.

At first, all I could see was blackness. "Hey— who's there?" My voice came out in a hushed whisper.

Will stepped out from the darkness. "Grady— it's you!" he cried. He came closer. He was wearing a dark sweatshirt over black jeans.

"Will—what are you *doing* out here?" I asked breathlessly.

"I heard the howls," he replied. "I decided to investigate."

"Me, too. I'm so glad to see you!" I exclaimed. "We can explore together."

"I'm glad to see you, too," he said. "It was so dark, I—I didn't know it was you. I thought—"

"I'm following Wolf," I told him. I led the way into the swamp. It grew even darker as we made our way under the low trees.

As we walked, I told Will about the night

before, about the murdered deer, the paw prints around the deer pen. I told him about how people in town were talking. And about how my dad planned to take Wolf away to the pound.

"I know Wolf isn't the killer," I told him. "I just know it. But Cassie got me so scared with all her werewolf stories, and—"

"Cassie is a jerk," Will muttered. He pointed into the weeds. "Look—there's Wolf!"

I could see his black outline moving steadily through the heavy darkness. "I was so stupid. I should have brought a torch," I murmured.

Wolf disappeared behind the weeds. Will and I followed the sound of his footsteps. We walked for several minutes. Suddenly, I realized I could no longer hear the dog.

"Where's Wolf?" I whispered, my eyes searching the dark bushes and low trees. "I don't want to lose him."

"He went this way," Will called back to me. "Follow me."

Our trainers slid over the damp, marshy ground. I slapped at a mosquito on the back of my neck. Too late. I could feel warm blood.

Deeper into the swamp. Past the bog, eerily silent now.

"Hey, Will?"

I stopped—and searched. "Oh." A soft cry escaped my lips as I realized I had lost him.

Somehow we had got separated.

I heard rustling up ahead. The crack of twigs. The whispering brush of weeds being stepped on and pushed out of the way.

"Will? Is that you?"

Or was it Wolf?

"Will?"

"Where *are* you?"

Pale light suddenly washed over me, washed slowly over the ground. Glancing up, I saw the heavy clouds pull away. The yellow full moon hovered high in the sky.

As the light slowly swept over the swamp, a low structure came into view straight ahead of me.

At first, I couldn't work out what it was. Some kind of gigantic plant?

No.

As the moonlight shone down, I realized I was staring at the swamp hermit's shack.

I stopped, frozen in sudden fear.

And then the howls began.

The frightening sound tore through the heavy silence. A horrifying wail, so loud, so nearby, rose on the still air, rose and then fell.

The sound was so terrifying, I raised my hands to cover my ears.

The swamp hermit! I thought. He *is* a werewolf!

I *knew* he was the werewolf!

115

I've got to get away from here, I realized. I've got to get home.

I turned away from the small shack.

My legs were trembling so hard, I didn't know if I could walk.

Got to go! Got to go! Got to go! The words repeated in my mind.

But before I could move, the werewolf burst out from behind a tree—and, howling its hideous howl, leapt on to my shoulders and shoved me to the ground.

As the yellow light of the full moon shone down, I gazed into the face of the werewolf as it pinned me to the ground.

Its dark eyes glared out at me from a human face, a human face covered in wolf fur. It howled its rage, its animal snout opening wide to reveal two gleaming rows of wolf fangs.

It's a human wolf! I realized to my terror. *A werewolf!*

"Get off!" I shrieked. "Will—get off me!"

It was Will. The werewolf was Will.

Even through the thick, matted wolf fur, I could recognize his dark features, his small, black eyes, his thick, stubby neck.

"Will—!" I screamed.

I struggled to push him away, to squirm out from under him.

But he was too powerful. I couldn't move.

"Will—*get off!*"

He raised his fur-covered face to the moon and

uttered an animal howl. Then, snarling out his rage, he lowered his beastly head and dug his fangs into my shoulder.

I let out a shriek of pain.

Blinding flashes of red filled my eyes.

I thrust out my hands, kicked my legs— struggled blindly to free myself.

But he had animal strength. He was much too strong for me . . . too strong . . . .

The flashing red faded, turned to black. Everything was fading to black. I could feel myself sinking, sinking down a black tunnel, sinking forever into deep, deep, endlessly deep darkness.

A loud growl brought me back.

Bewildered, I gazed up to see Wolf leap on to Will.

Will uttered a shrill howl of anger and turned to wrestle with the snarling dog.

I watched in stunned disbelief as they scrabbled over the ground, biting and clawing, raging at each other, growling and grunting.

"Will . . . Will, it was you . . . it was you all along. . . ." I murmured, struggling to my feet.

I gripped a tree trunk. The ground appeared to be sliding beneath me.

The two creatures continued to battle, grunting and growling as they clawed at each other, wrestling over the wet ground.

118

"I knew it wasn't Wolf," I muttered aloud. "I knew . . ."

And then a deafening high-pitched shriek startled me, and I tumbled to my knees.

I looked up in time to see Will running away, fleeing on all fours through the tall weeds. Wolf followed close behind, snapping at Will's ankles, jumping on him, biting and clawing him as they ran.

Then, I heard Will utter another cry of pain, a wail of defeat.

As the anguished sound faded, I sank down, down, down into the blue-black darkness.

"You have a slight temperature," Mum said. "But you'll be okay."

"Swamp fever," I murmured weakly. I gazed up at her, trying to focus. Her face was blurred, hovering over me in the soft light.

It took me a long while to realize I was in my own bedroom. "How—how did I get here?" I stammered.

"The swamp hermit—he found you in the swamp and carried you home," Mum said.

"He did?" I tried to sit up, but my shoulder ached. To my surprise, it was tightly bandaged. "The—the werewolf—Will—he bit me," I said, swallowing hard.

Dad's face hovered beside Mum's. "What are you saying, Grady? Why do you keep muttering about a werewolf?"

I pulled myself up a little and told them the whole story. They listened in silence, glancing at each other from time to time as I talked.

"Will is a werewolf," I concluded. "He changed. Under the full moon. He changed into a wolf, and—"

"I'm going to check this out right now," Dad said, staring intently down at me. "Your story is crazy, Grady. Just crazy. Maybe it's the fever. I don't know. But I'm going right over to your friend's house and see what's what."

"Dad—be careful," I called after him. "Be careful."

Dad returned a short while later, a bewildered look on his face. I was sitting in the living room, feeling a lot better, a big bowl of popcorn on my lap.

"There's no one there," Dad said, scratching his head.

"Huh? What do you mean?" Mum asked.

"The house is empty," Dad told us. "Deserted. It doesn't look like anyone has lived there for months!"

"Wow, Grady. You certainly have strange friends!" Emily exclaimed, rolling her eyes.

"I don't get it," Dad said, shaking his head.

I didn't, either. But I didn't care. Will was gone. The werewolf was gone for good.

"So can I keep Wolf?" I asked Dad, climbing up from the chair and crossing the room to him. "Wolf saved my life. Can I keep him?"

Dad stared back at me thoughtfully, but didn't reply.

"The swamp hermit told us he saw the dog chase some kind of animal away from Grady," Mum said.

"Probably a squirrel," Emily joked.

"Emily, give me a break," I groaned. "Wolf really saved my life," I told them.

"I suppose you can keep him," Dad said reluctantly.

"Hooray!" I thanked him and eagerly made my way to the back garden to give Wolf a happy hug.

That all happened nearly a month ago.

Since then, Wolf and I have had a wonderful time exploring the swamp. I've got to know just about every inch of Fever Swamp. It's like my second home.

Sometimes Wolf and I let Cassie come along to explore with us. She's sort of fun, even though she's always on the lookout for werewolves. I really wish she'd just drop the subject.

I'm standing at my bedroom window now, watching the full moon rising over the distant trees. This first full moon in a month makes me think of Will.

Will may be gone, but he changed my life. I know I'll never forget him.

I can feel the fur sprouting on my face. My

snout is expanding, and my fangs are sliding out between my dark lips.

Yes, when he bit me, Will passed the curse on to me.

But I don't mind. I'm not upset.

I mean, with Will out of the way, the swamp is now mine! All mine!

I'm climbing out of my window now. There's Wolf waiting for me, eager to do some night exploring.

I drop easily to the ground on all fours. I raise my fur-covered face to the moon and utter a long, joyful howl.

Let's go, Wolf. Let's hurry to Fever Swamp.

I'm ready to hunt.

Hippo Fantasy

Lose yourself in a whole new world, a world where anything is possible – from wizards and dragons, to time travel and new civilizations . . . Gripping, thrilling, scary and funny by turns, these Hippo Fantasy titles will hold you captivated to the very last page.

The Night of Wishes
Michael Ende (author of *The Neverending Story*)

It's New Year's Eve, and Beelzebub Preposteror, sorceror and evil-doer, has only seven hours to complete his annual share of villainous deeds and *completely destroy the world!*

Rowan of Rin
Emily Rodda

The witch Sheba has made a mysterious prophecy, which is like a riddle. A riddle Rowan must solve if he is to find out the secret of the mountain and save Rin from disaster . . .

The Wednesday Wizard
Sherryl Jordan

Denzil, humble apprentice to the wizard Valvasor, is in a real pickle. When he tries to reach his master to warn him of a dragon attack, he mucks up the spell and ends up seven centuries into the future!

The Practical Princess
Jay Williams

The Practical Princess has the gift of common sense. And when you spend your days tackling dragons and avoiding marriage to unsuitable suitors, common sense definitely comes in useful!